A LITTLE GETAWAY

A LITTLE GETAWAY

A SPICY SUSPENSE THRILLER

BONNIE TRAYMORE

First Edition
Honolulu, Hawai'i
Pathways Publishing
Print ISBN 979-8-218-49512-1

ALSO BY BONNIE TRAYMORE

Killer Motives

Little Loose Ends

Head Case

The Stepfamily

The Guest House

The Bluff

For Rick
Your secret's safe with me

PART 1

ONE

MORGAN

I smell death in the air. A briny scent with an undercurrent of decay, wafting in from the murky sea outside our sliding glass door.

"Kyle?" I call out again.

Nothing.

Maybe he went for a walk on the beach?

But that wasn't the plan.

Something's not right.

I close the door and lock it.

Where did he go?

A log pops in the fireplace, and I startle. This was supposed to be a romantic little getaway, but so far, things have been tense.

"I have a surprise for you, Morgan," he said, about a week ago.

So here I am, in this little cottage on the beach that he picked for us, in the middle of nowhere, a few miles north of Monterey Bay. A chance to rekindle our marriage. Put some spark back into it. The resort, if you could call it that, is a series of separate units on a vast swath of beachfront land, one step up from a trailer park. I suppose it could be romantic under different circumstances, with the rugged beach outside our door and a cozy fire inside.

I have a bad feeling, though. I came out of the shower and saw a few drops of blood in the bathroom sink. I figured he'd cut himself shaving. And now he's nowhere to be found. A chill runs up my spine. This place is getting creepier by the minute. Do I wait here like a sitting duck?

The office is on the other side of the property, and I'm not sure if anyone's there at this hour of the night. It's not that late. Just after nine in the evening. But even when we checked in, around noon, it took a good twenty minutes for the woman to come to the front desk and help us.

I don't want to overreact, so I decide I'll take the car and drive to the store.

Better safe than sorry.

We talked about the fact that I needed milk for my morning coffee. It'll buy me some time, and when I get back, maybe he'll be here, wondering where I've been. And if it turns out to be nothing, I can keep this little freak out to myself.

But we took his car, so I have to find the keys. I rush into the bedroom and look around. I thought I saw them on the dresser, but they're not there.

His pants are draped over the back of a chair.

I check the pockets.

Nothing.

My heart starts to race.

I rifle through his carry-on bag.

No luck.

His cell is gone, along with his wallet. I wonder if he went out for provisions while I was in the shower? But the car is parked near the office, a few cottages away, so I can't see if he's taken it. I pick up the house phone and call the front desk, thinking maybe the attendant could check if the car is there. It rings and rings and nobody answers.

My heart races even faster. Rushing into the kitchen area, I survey the options. I grab the utility knife. With its five-inch blade, it's the best option. This is a risky move. I'll look like a psycho walking around with it if someone sees me, and the last thing I want is to call attention to myself. But the place seems deserted, so it's unlikely I'll be spotted.

Who comes to a beach resort in the middle of winter?

This was his idea, I remind myself.

And now I'm here.

Alone.

At a deserted resort.

Clenching the knife in my fist, I step out the sliding glass door and start making my way to the front office.

TWO
MORGAN

The night is inky black. A bright crescent moon hangs in the sky, a bit too low. It sets me off balance, as if I'm dreaming. One of those realistic dreams, where everything seems normal.

Until it's not.

Gentle waves lick the shoreline, ebbing and flowing in a rhythmic dance that slows my racing heart. I take a deep breath and rethink this. Perhaps he's left me high and dry. Decided to skip out on me and disappear.

But I grip the knife in my hand, just in case.

I'm in danger.

I can feel it.

Someone comes at me from behind.

Instinctively, I whip my head around.

A black rubber mask hides his face and hair. He grabs my shoulders, spins me around, and stuffs a cloth in my face. It's damp, with some kind of liquid on it. I struggle to breathe as he presses it against my nose and mouth. I feel myself starting to fade.

Summoning my strength, I elbow him in the gut. He stumbles, giving me an opening. I could stab him in the leg, but that won't be fatal. He could get hold of the knife and use it on me. He's much stronger than I am.

I propel myself forward, hike up my knee, whip around, and slam it into his groin. He lets out a guttural moan and releases his grip.

It's not my first time.

I run for my life, realizing that I'm still clutching the knife in my hand. As I make my way to the office, I toss it into the bushes.

I whip open the door. Thankfully, they didn't lock it yet.

"Hello!" I call out.

I press the bell, over and over and over.

Ding.

Ding.

Ding.

Ding.

A fifty-something man with a large frame and a lumbering gait rubs his eyes as he meanders out from the door behind the front desk.

"What's so urgent at this hour of the night?" he says.

"My husband is missing," I say, catching my breath. He eyes me, brow furrowed, as if he's about to protest. "And someone just tried to kill me."

His jaw drops and he stands there, immobilized.

"Lock the door!" I command, adrenaline coursing through my veins.

He fumbles around for the keys in a drawer.

I want to smack him. My eyes widen. "Hurry up!" I cry out.

He rushes over to the front door and locks us in, and I call for help.

"TELL ME AGAIN WHAT HAPPENED," she says.

The officer is a sturdy-looking woman with short dark hair and a serious face. Maybe forty? A bit older than me. Her expression isn't mean or menacing. More like determined. She told me her name, but it went in one ear and out the other.

I'm relieved it's a woman, because I feel like she might actually believe me. I've watched a few Netflix documentaries recently about detectives who turn victims into suspects, and I can only hope I'm not the next one. As I said, we've been having marital problems, and that never looks good in a missing persons case. Kyle's car is gone, and so is he. That's all I know about what happened to him, and I tell her so.

We've been over it once, but I start from the beginning.

"So, you came out of the shower. What time was that?"

"About nine o'clock," I say.

"And then what happened?"

"I looked around and he wasn't there. So, I called out to him and there was no answer. I checked the sliding glass door and it was locked from the inside, so I knew he wasn't out for a walk."

That's a lie.

"I went to look for his keys, thinking that maybe he went out to get milk."

The officer sits back and cocks her head to one side as she holds my gaze.

"For my coffee," I offer. "We'd talked about the fact that I'd need to get it in the morning. I thought maybe he'd gone out to get it. To surprise me. But I couldn't find his keys. And then I got nervous. I decided to go to the front desk and see if he'd taken the car, and if not, I was going to call for help."

Her brow furrows. "I feel like I'm missing something here," she says. "It's nine forty-five now. He couldn't have been gone for very long. If you couldn't find the keys, why didn't you wait longer? Why did you jump to conclusions? Why did you feel like something was wrong?"

My stomach sinks.

I swallow. "Um, I saw those drops of blood in the sink. Then I tried to call him, and he didn't answer."

Crap.

Another lie.

"I mean, the call didn't go through. The cell service is spotty here. So, I headed to the office to see if I could get through to him. And to see if he'd taken the car somewhere."

She nods.

I take a deep breath.

There's an uncomfortable silence.

"And now his cell goes straight to voicemail." She states it as a fact, not a question, but I answer her anyway.

"Yes," I confirm.

"Now, tell me about this attacker," she says.

I repeat what I told her the first time, more confident about this part. Someone attacked me, and I'm not letting them turn this around on me.

"And you didn't see his face?" she says.

"No. He had on a black rubber mask. It covered his face and hair."

"Eye color?" she asks.

I sigh. "It was too dark."

She eyes me, one brow above the other, as if she's skeptical. "And you fought the guy off?" She smirks. "Lucky break."

I'm on the petite side, with a girl-next-door look that belies my inner strength. I've been told I look a little like Kristen Bell, and I know it's hard to believe I could fight off a pro like the guy who tried to kill me.

"It's not luck," I say. "I've had some training."

Her head tilts. I've become a curiosity to her.

"I learned my lesson. Years ago." I take a deep breath and look away. Then I turn back to her. "But I'd rather not talk about that right now."

That's not a lie, and she seems to sense it.

She nods and her face softens, as if she understands me now. "We'll take you down to the station, Ms. Murphy, and we can file a missing persons report. After we've finished up our investigation. You live where again?"

"Saratoga. It's about a two-hour drive. And I don't have a car."

"We'll find a way to get you home. Don't worry about that."

But I am worried.

Because someone tried to kidnap me. This wasn't a

random burglary. Everything's falling apart. I have no idea where Kyle is, and my life is in danger.

But one step at a time.

For now, the police are on my side.

And I don't know how long that will last.

THREE

MORGAN

ONE MONTH EARLIER

Kyle and I have never had what you'd call a typical marriage. But it's always been hot. And we haven't had sex in over a week. Something's up with him, I can feel it. We met over ten years ago, when I was still in my twenties. He's five years older than me, which is just about perfect. I'm a paralegal, and he was one of our clients. A real estate developer who got himself into a jam with the city planning commission.

We cleared it up for him, and he was eternally grateful. I'm actually the one who found the loophole. I'm much smarter than I let on. The cute little blonde act is a good cover, because when I go for the jugular, nobody sees it coming.

I could have done more with my life, and maybe I should have. But I saw what it was like for women like me, trying to have it all, and decided it wasn't for me. My first boss was a creep, and he got what was coming to him. But that's a story for another time. Let's just say it put me off the corporate track. That was before the #MeToo movement, and although that's made an impact, it's still not even close to a level playing field for women. And besides, if I made it to the top, people might just assume I'd slept my way there.

So, I decided a better strategy would be to tether myself to a powerful man. I never expected to fall head over heels in love. That was a bonus. I didn't know I could feel like that about anyone. And now Kyle is cooling to me, and I have to find out why.

I swear, my blood boils just thinking about him with another woman. If he's cheating on me, I don't know if I could contain my rage. It simmers, just below the surface, and it's never erupted full steam. I worry, because I don't want to go to prison. I've never killed anyone, but I have done some damage—but only to people who deserved what they got. There's no telling what I might do if I caught him in the act.

Calm down, I tell myself. Maybe it's something else, knowing my husband. I knew from the start that Kyle wasn't above bending the rules to get what he wanted. I liked that about him. I wanted an alpha male. The kind of guy who would march into the jungle and bring me back a fresh catch of meat, eliminating anyone who stood in his way.

He doesn't tell me much about his dealings, but I've got my ways of keeping track of him. There's one investor of his I'm worried about, so I'll start there. Perhaps he's gotten himself into some kind of trouble, and I can help us figure a way out.

Kyle left earlier than usual this morning, and so I'm a little ahead of schedule. My profession comes in handy at times like this, especially if I can beat everyone in and have the place to myself for a while to dig into the databases.

Forgoing a second cup of coffee, I gather my things and head out.

———

I MOVED to another law firm when Kyle and I got together, but I've gleaned enough information from working on his case to know where to start. I'm just about to dig in when one of the junior partners comes barging into my office, interrupting me. What's he doing here so early? There's so much toxic masculinity around here, I'm surprised I haven't grown chest hairs.

"Did you get that brief I left on your desk?" Roger asks.

Which means he hasn't checked his email today. Because I've not only read the brief, I've corrected it, added to it, and sent it off already. I tell him this. He offers me a sheepish smile but stops short of apologizing.

Roger's not the worst of the bunch. He looks like a giant baby. Big and fleshy, with a jolly face and a curly shock of brown hair. I cover for his blunders some of the time. *I think that guy was trying to pull his leg over my head.* He does this often. Mixes up his sayings. We call them Roger-isms. He gets away with being a bit of a goofball because clients like him. His saving grace is that he's a sports savant, and he can spew statistics like nobody's business. I guess that counts for a lot in the bro world.

I've got the upper hand in this relationship, and I could make a bigger deal out of the way he just treated me. But he's an ally, and I get what I need from him, so I don't make an issue of it.

"You're the best," he says.

I hold his gaze with a sinister half-smile until he starts to squirm. People don't realize the power of silence.

He lowers his eyes. "I'm sorry I didn't check before I bothered you, Morgan," he says. Then he slinks out of my office.

It's not hyperbole. I'm the best paralegal in this firm, and everyone knows it. But I still have to stay in my lane. The cute, efficient little blonde girl who comes to everyone's rescue.

If they only knew what I'm truly capable of.

"HEY, BABE," Kyle says, stopping to give me a long, languishing kiss as I put the finishing touches on our dinner. It's the kind of kiss that goes right to my lady parts, and it lights me up inside. I'm about to take it up a notch, but then I pull back. Partly because I've found that delaying the gratification of his wishes takes the hotness up to a whole other level. I like to wait until he's about to burst, because when he looks at me like a ravenous animal consumed with desire for me? Well, there's nothing quite like it.

But also because I'm now a bit suspicious of the timing. I started poking around in some of our financial accounts today. I can't help but wonder if he caught wind of it, and his renewed desire for me is some kind of cover, meant to deflect me from whatever he's trying to hide.

"Good day?" I ask.

"Really good one," he says.

He caresses my body and nuzzles the crook of my neck. Tingles shoot through me, but I push him away. We haven't eaten yet, and I feign concern about overcooked chicken. But the hunger in his eyes overpowers me, and I give in.

Maybe I was worried for nothing, and we'll finally get back to normal. I turn off the stove, and we grab at each other like the world is ending. He lifts up my skirt and attempts to hoist me up on the counter.

"The bedroom," I moan.

Because that kind of thing looks good in movies, but in reality, it's totally uncomfortable, and who needs that? Plus, I've realized over the years that the best way to get information out of my husband is to screw his brains out and leave him spent and defenseless. When he's lying in bed, staring up at the ceiling after a good roll in the hay, the floodgates open. It's when I feel the most connected to him; it's the only time he allows himself to be vulnerable with me.

He takes me by the hand with that ravenous look in his eyes, and I feel myself starting to tingle in all the right places. He spreads me out on the bed and strokes the inside of my thigh, making his way up and down my body, gently teasing me with everything in his arsenal. By the time he enters me, I'm lost in it. And then we lie there for a bit, spent and satiated.

I'm about to reach for him. Ask him straight out why he's been so distant, while he's in a post-roll-in-the-hay stupor, still so close to me, I can feel his sweat on my body and his breath in my ear.

But this time, after we finish, he springs up.

"I'm starved," he says.

Then he hops out of bed and smiles at me. "Let's eat."

I nearly break down and cry.

FOUR

MORGAN

THREE WEEKS EARLIER

I've made progress this week, and things are worse than I thought. Money is missing from two of our accounts, and my husband's been avoiding me. What the hell is going on? I've started following Kyle when I can, and it's turned up nothing of value. But there's only so much I can do on my own. I have a job. I can't follow him around all day.

Luckily, I have a mole on the inside. Her name is Carla Flores, and she's an accountant at Kyle's company. I don't have many girlfriends. I've always had a hard time with that. But she and I forged an alliance of sorts, years ago. We met ten years ago, when I was working on Kyle's case, and I know I can count on her to be discreet. She owes me one, and she's the type to pay her debts.

We're meeting in person. I'm not stupid enough to use email or my cell phone. If Kyle's up to something, the cops might be listening in. Carla's even more of a hothead than I am. Two years ago, she nearly ordered a hit on her husband

Eddie when she thought he was cheating on her. He'd been sneaking around. Hanging up the phone when she came into the room. Turns out he was planning a surprise trip to the Philippines to see her cousin and renew their wedding vows. We had a laugh about that one.

I'm waiting for her at a Thai place in downtown Saratoga she likes. Here she comes now, balanced on her spiky heels that click and clack on the tile floor. She's even smaller than me, with long, dark waves and an infectious smile.

"What's going on?" Carla asks, as she slides into the booth and sits down across from me.

I don't give her all the sordid details. I'm not one of those women who likes to divulge the juicy details of my sex life. But I tell her the basics. Things have cooled off. He's avoiding intimacy. Money seems to be missing from one of our stock accounts, and our checking account is lower than normal.

Her brow furrows. "Well, off the top of my head, I'd say he's in some kind of financial trouble. And he's avoiding intimacy because he thinks you'll pick up on it. But I'll keep an eye on him. Let you know if I see anything around the office."

We stop to order our food when the waiter arrives. A Thai salad for me, and tom yum talay, a pungent fish soup, for her. Then she fills me in on her kids. She's got two boys, five and eight. They keep her busy, but she doesn't complain. Kyle and I have never wanted kids, which most people don't understand.

Except for Carla. She never pries or asks us if we're

trying. Although she clearly loves her boys, I can't help but wonder if she doesn't miss the days when it was just the two of them, just a little. They're one of those madly-in-love couples.

Like we used to be.

"Do you want to hire a PI? I know a good one," Carla says.

Of course she does.

"A private investigator?"

She nods and sips her tea.

"No. Not yet. What if he's up to something illegal? I can't take that kind of a risk."

"Well, don't jump to conclusions," she says. "I say this from experience. I could have been a widow." She laughs; a hearty laugh that reverberates around the empty restaurant. "Eddie got a kick out of it."

I shake my head. "He's certainly got a strange sense of humor."

She shrugs. "He said it was like that movie. The one with Kevin Klein and Tracy Ullman. I forget the name. Do you know it?"

"*I Love You to Death*," I say. "It's based on a true story."

I know all the classic romance stories, and that one stayed with me. It was based on a real couple. The wife tried to kill her cheating husband by hiring a pair of thugs to shoot him in the head, but it didn't quite take. When the husband recovered and found out what had happened, he was so sorry about how much he'd hurt her, he vowed to be faithful until the end.

She nods. "I know. Did you know they're still together?"

"I heard," I say.

"Now that's true love. Like me and Eddie." She smiles.

I'm not sure I agree, but I smile back. "You two are made for each other, that's for sure."

The waiter places our lunches in front of us, and I put my napkin on my lap. Carla follows suit.

She takes a spoonful of steaming hot soup to her mouth, blows on it a few times, then sips it down. "So, what makes you think he's cheating?" she asks.

"Something's different, Carla. I can feel it." I take a bite of my salad, forcing myself to eat. "With Eddie, that time you were suspicious. Were things different? In the bedroom, I mean?"

Carla stares off to the side for a minute. "No." She shakes her head. "Not really, come to think of it. We were still us."

I let out a sigh. "I can tell you this. He's not planning some surprise party for me, that's for sure. Either he's cheating, or it's something even more dangerous for us. You know how he is. And I need to get ahead of it."

Carla pats my hand and looks me in the eye. "We'll figure it out. Don't worry."

I nod, and we both make progress on our meals.

"But let me ask you this," she says. "If he is cheating, what's your next move? Because if you don't have an answer to that question, maybe you're better off not knowing. Letting this blow over."

My stomach sinks. It's a good question, and my salad turns in my stomach as I ponder it. This is a slippery slope, and I very well may go sliding down it into a very dark place.

What if I catch him?

What's my next move?

Cheating is the ultimate betrayal for me. Kyle knows that. He knows how I feel about infidelity. In my book, it's worse than murder. Well, maybe not worse, but it's close.

I'm not Carla. I wouldn't order a hit on him.

I wouldn't let him off that easy.

I'd need to look him in the eye.

I've been at this for two weeks and here's what I know. One of Kyle's development projects has stalled. It's a residential condo building on the outskirts of Campbell that was zoned agricultural but was expected to be rezoned residential, part of an effort to build more affordable housing. But for some reason, the zoning change didn't go through. And now the project is in jeopardy.

That's one problem with my husband. He's an eternal optimist. Calling him a real estate developer is a stretch. He works for a commercial real estate firm in sales. But he does side deals, and this is one of those deals. His last one went well, and we could have left it at that. We have a lovely townhouse with hardly any mortgage in this small complex he developed a few years ago.

But he wanted more, and I can only imagine what he told the investors. Probably sold it as a sure thing. I wonder if he even told them that it was a high-risk situation. They've already ordered most of the supplies for the project, and now they're sitting in a warehouse, costing money instead of making it. Of course, he owns the land too, and unless he wants to become a farmer, it's basically worthless to us and his investors if the zoning change doesn't go through. Meanwhile, the commercial market has stalled, and his commissions have dwindled.

Kyle's from New York, where his family had a lot of influence. Brooklyn, to be precise, where there's a sprawling Murphy clan. He's so different from the guys around here. That's what attracted me to him. His accent has faded a bit but it's still noticeable, and it gets thicker when he's excited or agitated.

I imagine his Irish-American family had mob connections back in the day, but he never talks about it. There's an edge to him that I find alluring. But he doesn't have the connections here that he had back home, and the politics are different, so it doesn't surprise me that he's gotten himself into some trouble.

There's one investor I'm concerned about. Wes Walker. He owns a large wood supply company. Walker Wood and Lumber Supply. Kyle's done business with him before. I remember this from the last time Kyle had legal troubles, back when we met. This guy was one of his suppliers, and one of the attorneys at my old firm told me there were rumors about him. That he was possibly bringing in illegal timber—the third most prevalent transnational crime, and one that's tougher to prosecute than the others.

At that time, Walker was a supplier, not an investor. But now it seems as if he's invested in Kyle's condo development project. And if I'm right about him, he won't take too kindly to his investment evaporating into thin air. So far, Carla hasn't been able to find a money trail leading to him, but she called just now and said she has something for me. I can't imagine what else Kyle would be doing with that money. I'm at work, getting ready to leave for my lunch break and find out what she's got for me.

"Morgan," Candace Thompson says as she marches into my office. "I need your help with something."

Candace is one of the named partners here; she poached me from my last firm. She's tried to mentor me over the years. Encouraged me to think about law school. But I think she's finally given up. Still, she has my back around here, and I appreciate her support. I'm in a rush, but I can't come out and say that.

She hands me a file and tells me what she needs, and then I decide to be bold.

"Can it wait until after lunch?" I ask.

Candace bristles.

For a moment, I'm afraid I've overplayed my hand. They're all workaholics around here, and I get away with working a relatively sane number of hours because I'm good at what I do. But I can't push my luck.

"I've got a doctor's appointment," I add.

"Oh," she says.

She eyes me suspiciously, but she lets it go. HR has pushed back a bit on the principals for not being family friendly. "Sure. Do what you need to do, Morgan. But have it by end of day."

"You've got it," I say with a perky smile on my face, reminding myself that the firm trumps sisterhood. *Always.* She'll cut me loose in a heartbeat if she finds out I'm lying.

MY FIRM IS IN SUNNYVALE, and Carla works in downtown San Jose. We're meeting at Jollyman Park in Cupertino, but she's not here yet. It's a pleasant and sunny California winter day, close to sixty degrees, and I need some fresh air. The park has a nice walking path, some playground equipment, and mature trees that provide the perfect amount of shade.

I sit down at a picnic bench and take out my bagged lunch: a turkey and avocado sandwich on wheat bread. I'm not above brown bagging it. People around here have a lot of money, and I could feel poor by comparison. But I don't. I grew up in much more humble circumstances, and Kyle and I are very comfortable.

Carla arrives and takes a seat across from me. "I've got something. But don't go crazy, okay? It might not be what you think." She wags her finger at me as she takes the lid off her salad container.

"Just spill it, Carla," I say. "What's going on?"

"Kyle ducked out yesterday. And there was nothing on his calendar. I saw him looking around as he was leaving, like he didn't want to be seen. So I followed him."

"And?"

She pours some dressing on her salad, puts the lid back on, and shakes it. She takes it off, pours a little more, and mixes it with her fork. We don't have all day, but I resist the urge to snap at her for drawing this out.

"He went to a coffee shop near the office," she says, finally. "And he met someone there." She lets out a sigh. "Now don't freak out. It was a woman."

"I knew it!" I rest my head in my hands.

"Hold up," she says. "It might be nothing." She shovels a few forkfuls of salad into her mouth. I wait while she chews and swallows and takes a sip of her iced tea. "Sorry. I'm starved." Then she takes a bite of pita bread, chews, and swallows.

I tap my fingers on the tabletop. "And? What happened?" I ask, widening my eyes.

"I didn't see much. I was trying to be discreet. The woman waved him over, and he went and sat down. Then I left."

"What did she look like?" I ask.

"I didn't get a good look. She was sitting down. Mid-thirties, if I had to guess. Dark hair. Nothing special, from what I could see."

I'm sure she's just being kind. I pictured this moment many times over the last two weeks, thinking that if my suspicions turned out to be correct, my first emotion would be rage.

But I was wrong. A wave of nausea grips me, and bile rises in my throat. Kyle's the only man who's had my back since my father died when I was small. The only one who knows what I've been through. He's all I have, and he knows that. It took years to build trust, and the fact that he would throw it all away shakes me to my core. My stomach churns and I find myself getting choked up, which is the last thing I need.

"We need more information, Morgan," she says. "Don't assume the worst. She could be a business associate. They didn't hug or kiss or anything."

"He's not stupid. They were in a public place. What was

the body language like? Were they sitting back or leaning in?" My stomach tenses, and I'm not sure I want to hear the answer.

She takes a breath and blows it out. "Leaning in," she says. "But that doesn't mean—"

I hold up my palm. "Leaning in! I know what that means. This is bad," I say. "He's cheating on me. I can tell by the way things have cooled off at home." At some point, I expect the pain I'm feeling will be replaced by a murderous rage, but I'm not there yet.

"Let me get more proof, okay? We don't know enough yet. Promise me you'll try to keep your cool."

"I'll try, but I'm not making any promises it'll work."

"Good girl. I'm not sure how much I can get without engaging a professional. Are you sure you don't want to talk to that PI I know? Shep Shackler?"

"Shep Shackler? What kind of name is that?"

She shrugs. "He's good."

"No. I told you. We need to keep this between us. I can't trust anyone else with this."

"What about tracking his cell phone?"

"No. We've got different systems. He's Android. I'm not."

"How about a GPS tracker?"

"That might work."

She tells me which brand to buy. A small one that attaches with a magnet. "He'll never notice it," she says.

"Are you speaking from experience?" I ask.

"Guilty." She smirks. "But the battery runs down fast if you track it constantly, so you'll need to be selective. If it's on all the time, it'll last about a week."

"Thanks for the tip, Carla. Have you thought about working for the CIA?"

She shoots me a look. "Okay, so, in the event he really is cheating, what's your next move?" she asks.

That's the million-dollar question.

"I don't know yet."

But it won't be pretty.

SIX

MORGAN

TWO WEEKS EARLIER

I came home early for the first time in the nearly six years I've worked at the firm. Candace took one look at me with my puffy eyes and figured I'd gotten some terrible diagnosis. She told me to take the afternoon off.

Maybe she's not so bad, after all.

The anger is bubbling up now, and I can't sit still. I went to the gym and blew off some steam, but I'm still hopped up, pacing around the house. And I can't see how I'll be able to feign normalcy when Kyle gets home.

I forced myself to eat something. I've always had trouble keeping weight on, and I know that sounds like a good problem to have. But men like curves, and I don't have them. As a teen, I was mousy and flat-chested, with braces until my junior year of high school. Not the kind of girl who got a lot of attention from guys, which was somewhat intentional; my stepdad was a creep.

As an adult, I've learned to play up my assets, and I know that I turn heads now with my blonde bob and my long, shapely legs that I've managed to craft with regular weight training. But I've always envied the voluptuous types, and I wonder if some *Playboy* centerfold wannabe is presently trying to steal my husband. I hate that my insecurities still haunt me. You'd think I'd be over it by now.

I try to fuel myself with anger and suppress the sadness and doubt, but I can't tap into it yet. It will come, though, and God help Kyle when it does. But I need to play the long game. As Carla said, it could be something else. We don't have any proof yet.

So, I take a deep breath, flip open my computer, and get to work, digging into Wes Walker and his business. If he's a threat to us, I need to get ahead of it. He invested close to a million in Kyle's project, by far the single biggest investor. If it weren't for him, Kyle would never have gotten that construction loan. Walker's not on the hook for the loan, though, so that's the good news.

But if he wants his money back, where can we get a million dollars?

KYLE CALLED and said he'd be late. He's having dinner with a client. Who has dinner with a client these days? What a load of crap. I'm nobody's pushover, and Kyle's going to find that out the hard way. That reminds me, I need to order that GPS tracker. Logging on to my computer, I find the brand Carla recommended and order it. My stomach tenses at the thought of what I might uncover about my husband's secret life.

But Kyle's not the only one with secrets in this house.

There are parts I left out of my story, and even Kyle doesn't know everything there is to know about me. My father was my world when I was a child. My mother had problems. Emotional issues. And he tried to shield me from them. That much he knows.

After my father died, when I was seven, it was my mom and me for two years. After a gut-wrenching few months, she pulled herself together. And it wasn't so bad, although we both missed him terribly. She was a bookkeeper, and we struggled financially. I was a latchkey kid, and that was fine with me. We were middle class, back when middle class meant comfortable, not struggling to survive. We lived in Morgan Hill until she remarried.

Morgan from Morgan Hill.

My stepdad used to say that when he was at a loss for words, kind of like a verbal tic. I hear his voice in my head now, and it makes my stomach turn.

Hey, Morgan from Morgan Hill.

How's Morgan from Morgan Hill today?

He was an accountant who seemed to be the answer to all of our problems. Dorky. Awkward around me. But he made a good living, and we moved into a nicer home. His home in Campbell, and he never let me forget it. He didn't have any kids, so I was still an only child.

A year or so after I hit puberty, he started looking at me differently. One day, when I was fourteen, I was slicing up some veggies, prepping for dinner before my mother came home from work. He came up behind me, startling me. I didn't know he was home.

He rested his right hand on the island countertop and leaned his body over mine. I could feel his breath on my neck, and it made my skin crawl. He started to caress my shoulder with his left hand. I let it go for a minute, to lull him into a false sense of security. As his left hand meandered around toward my breast and rested on it, I plunged the knife into his right thumb, which was still firmly planted on the countertop.

He let out a howling cry, the knife still stuck in his flesh. I watched as the blood seeped out over the cutting board, mixing with the broccoli and carrots. Bright red and orange and green, swirling together on the white countertop.

I pulled out the knife. He shrunk back from me, like I was some kind of demon child.

What did he expect?

Men like him need to learn.

He drove himself to the hospital. Told my mother he'd cut himself making dinner. We never spoke of it again. I didn't have any further issues with him, at least in that department. He looked a little like Ned Flanders on *The Simpsons*. Needless to say, he totally ruined the show for me.

When I told Kyle this story, about a year before we got married, I left out the part where I stabbed him. I didn't tell Kyle about the stabbing because I thought it might worry him. That it might put him off me. Instead, I said I slapped him in the face.

"Good for you, Morgs," Kyle said. "Next time, kick 'em in the balls."

And right now, I'm glad I didn't tell him the whole story. Because my husband doesn't know what I'm capable of, and if I choose to get even with Kyle, he won't see it coming.

I TOOK a sedative to calm myself down and went to bed early. I thought I'd need to feign sleep, but I must have knocked myself out. Kyle's next to me, fast asleep. His mouth is open a little, and he's been making a whistling, wheezy noise. That's probably what woke me. It's just after three in the morning.

I watch as his chest rises and falls. In the looks department, Kyle's a bit of an acquired taste. He's not the guy you swoon over when you walk into a room. I didn't want a guy like that. They're trouble. But he's handsome and funny, and he knows his way around a woman. Although he's of average height and build, he has a commanding presence. His rakish smile sets me on fire every time he flashes it at me, like we're sharing a secret that we hide from the world. He hasn't looked at me like that for a few weeks now, and I'm going to find out why.

I sneak out of bed and head downstairs. We live in a townhome, and it's more than enough for the two of us. Three bedrooms, two and a half baths. A nice view of the mountains in the distance from our bedroom. I head into our kitchen, which is state-of-the-art. Kyle didn't spare any expenses when he built these units. The cabinets are made of cherry wood stained a dark brown shade, with off-white granite countertops and thin subway tile backsplashes that mirror the wood grain. It's a chef's kitchen. Wolf gas range, Sub-Zero fridge made of stainless steel and glass. We really should entertain more often.

After I get some coffee, I start combing through his briefcase. There's some paperwork for his development project from the planning commission. Kyle's apparently trying to appeal the decision on the rezoning. Then I see a manila envelope from an insurance company. It's not sealed, so I open it and take out the papers.

Life insurance?

My stomach sinks.

Kyle's increasing our life insurance. Two million dollars on each of us.

Why do we need this much insurance?

We don't have kids, and we have hardly any mortgage. Why would he increase it?

I can think of one reason. He's planning to kill me. To get himself out of debt and clear the way for the next Mrs. Murphy. But he's increasing it on both of us, and that's his first mistake. Because I now know one thing for sure. My husband's worth more to me dead than alive.

And if he's cheating, I'm going to strike first.

A strange calm has come over me, and it's not what I expected. I thought when I had more proof, I'd flip into a rage. But I haven't.

At least not yet.

Earlier this week, Carla followed Kyle when he ducked out of the office again. She snapped a photo of him heading into the Westin, a downtown hotel walking distance from his office. And this time, she was able to wait. And she also snapped a photo of the same woman from the coffee shop, coming out of the hotel about an hour later, ten minutes before Kyle exited the building.

I'm looking at it now. She's about my age. A brunette, wearing her long hair in a messy ponytail. Maybe Kyle wanted a little variety. She's not dressed in a way to attract attention. Slacks and a blouse, with a suit jacket folded over her arm. Professional, like she's coming from work. But no briefcase. She's got a nice shape. And full, pouty lips with an olive complexion. I think about what Carla said, about not jumping to conclusions. But what else would they be doing in a hotel room in the middle of the day?

Perhaps he joined a dating site for married people. Like those people who claim they're happily married but need a little variety on the side. Maybe ten years is too long for monogamy for a guy like Kyle, no matter how hard we try to keep it spicy. He joked about a threesome once, about a year or so ago, when we were watching some TV show about a couple who'd tried it.

"What'ya think, Morgan? Wanna give it a go?" He gave me a tickle.

"Ha! I'd scratch her eyes out the minute she laid a hand on you," I said.

Kyle laughed and hugged me closer. But maybe it wasn't a joke to him. Maybe he was feeling me out, and I wouldn't go far enough for him, and this is where it led. To a hotel, in the middle of a workday.

Not that I'm blaming myself. I may be sexually adventurous in my marriage, but I'm a zealot about monogamy, and I think people who say they're okay with threesomes and open marriages and all that malarky are kidding themselves. I *would* scratch her eyes out, too, I'm pretty sure of it. Even if she was a nice person. And any woman who wouldn't is probably sick of the guy she's with. Jealousy is a natural, primal reaction, encoded in our DNA.

Meanwhile, I can tell by the GPS tracker I put on my husband's car that he's had two meetings with Wes Walker this week, and I know that something's wrong. He cashed in some stock about a week ago and withdrew fifty grand before he went over there the second time. From the looks of it, the project has them much more in the hole than that. At least a million dollars, or more. We don't have that kind of money.

But we do have life insurance.

Lots of it.

He asked me to sign the paperwork last week to increase its value. Made up some excuse about wanting to up the amount because two of his projects had increased our net worth, including the one that's stalled. He brushed the delay off as a temporary setback, assuring me that he had it under control, and that he was working on a fix with a local representative.

The woman in the photo is dressed like a politician or a bureaucrat, so for a short time, I thought maybe I had it wrong. I did an internet search and looked up anyone and everyone who could be involved in the rezoning issue, but none of the photos were a match. And again, why would they meet up at a hotel?

So now I'm back to my suspicions about an affair. I'm sure Kyle knows that I'm up to something. We've been off lately. Like two ships passing in the night. Polite and awkward around each other. And as much as I want to be angry, I miss him terribly.

I wander around our home, thinking of all the good times. We're the kind of couple who keep to ourselves most of the time. Even when we're out with friends, having a good time, we sneak looks at each other, itching to get home and be alone, together.

Not so long ago, we were out with another couple. One of his investor friends and his wife. About halfway through dinner, he pressed a note in my palm, instructing me to meet him in the bathroom in five minutes.

I can't wait until we get home, he mouthed, and he slipped out.

I excused myself a few minutes later and headed to the restroom area, but I didn't know which door he was behind. It was one of those trendy spots that had a bunch of single occupancy bathrooms, with a row of sinks outside to wash your hands. On the second knock, I found him.

He pulled me in, and we giggled like a pair of teenagers who'd ducked out of math class. He hoisted me up and I wrapped my legs around him, my heart racing and my loins burning for him. When we came back to the table, flushed and breathless, I'm sure the other couple knew where we'd been. But I didn't care.

We were *that couple*.

The one that everyone envied.

The couple who never grew tired of each other.

Where every day was an adventure.

That's what makes this so hard.

How could he do this to me?

I'M in the living room when Kyle comes home.

Late.

Again.

He texted earlier and said not to wait for him for dinner.

I've had friends whose marriages have gone south. And I always wondered how they let it happen. I mean, why not just talk to the person? But now I see how it is when things start to go bad. The rhythm is all off, and it seems like anything you say just makes it worse. It's heartbreaking.

What used to be effortless and light is heavy and dense, like lead balls in my stomach.

"Babe," he says. "How was your day?"

I'm lying on the sofa, reading. A rom-com that I thought would make me happy, but it's making me more depressed. I don't look up.

"Fine," I say, turning the page.

He sits down near my feet, and I scrunch up my legs.

"Morgan," he says.

"Yes?" I stop reading and give him my attention.

"I know things have been a little... tense lately."

Maybe he'll finally come clean. Tell me about the issues he's having with the project. Let me in. For a brief moment, I have hope that things might go back to normal.

"I've been busy, and I know I haven't been very attentive."

He thinks this is about me?

That I'm craving attention?

Clenching my teeth, I fight to stay calm.

"But I've got a lot wrapped up in the new project, and I'm excited about it."

I'm steaming, but I take a deep breath and play along. "Well, you have been a bit distant. How's the project going?" I ask.

This should be good.

"Great," he says. "It's going just great. We should break ground soon."

That's total bullshit.

I can feel my pulse start to pound. He's flat out lying to me about the project. "Really?" I reply. "That was fast. I thought you said it would take a while."

"I got it all figured out, babe. Don't worry about it. And I have a surprise for you."

"A surprise?"

He flashes me his rakish grin, and I want to smack it off his face.

"A little getaway. Just the two of us. Next weekend. It's this cozy beach resort on the coast. About two hours south. I know you love the beach. It'll be quiet and romantic. It'll give us a chance to get our mojo back."

He reaches for my foot and squeezes it.

And it's then that I smell it.

It's subtle. Not too overpowering. Perfect Veil, by Sarah Horowitz, if I had to guess. I have a nose like a bloodhound. It's not a big claim to fame, but it comes in handy at times like this. "Sounds great, Kyle." I turn from him and go back to my book.

He sits there for a while, waiting to see if I'll engage, but I ignore him. After a few minutes, he heads upstairs.

I love the beach in Mexico or the Caribbean, not in Northern California in the winter. But I don't mention that. Because it's clear to me what's going on. My husband took out a two-million-dollar life insurance policy on me, he's been seeing some mystery woman whose perfume now clings to him, he owes money to a dangerous man, and now he's taking me to a secluded beach resort in the middle of winter. It doesn't take a genius to connect these dots.

It's time for me to go on the offensive.

EIGHT

MORGAN

PRESENT DAY

"We've got blood, Martinez." A young male officer interrupts us, poking his head into the lobby. The female officer I'm sitting with springs up.

"Call for backup," she says to him. "Wait here," she barks at me. "Don't go anywhere. Understand?"

I nod, and she rushes out the door. At least I've got a name now. Officer Martinez and I were just getting to know each other. And I'm more confused than ever.

Could it be Kyle's blood?

But that wasn't the plan. So, if someone took him, it had nothing to do with me. And now they're after me. Then I think about the knife I ditched. If they find it in the bushes, which they will, it'll have my prints on it. I need to get it before that happens.

But how?

I can't do it now. They'll see me. But as soon as they check the unit, they'll see that one of the knives is missing.

And the hotel must have some kind of video surveillance. They'll see it in my hand.

I decide it's better to get ahead of it. I sit, sweating bullets, waiting for Officer Martinez to return, while competing fears swirl in my head. Fear that someone wants to kill me. Fear that they'll figure out what I was planning to do to Kyle, and I'll go to prison. Good thing I took the GPS tracker off his car before we came down here. And, although I hate to admit it, fear that someone has Kyle, doing God knows what to him.

And now I'm starting to have regrets about how I handled this. I should have confronted Kyle about the money and the mystery woman. We could have figured something out together. Maybe he wasn't cheating. And now I may have lost him forever.

After about fifteen minutes, she comes back.

"What's happening?" I ask. "Do you think something's happened to my husband?"

"We'll have to test the blood. I'll need something with his DNA."

"I've got his toothbrush back in the room. And those blood drops in the sink."

She nods.

"But I forgot to tell you something," I say.

She narrows her eyes at me. "What's that?"

"There's a knife in the bushes, just outside the lobby entrance. I took it from the unit, when I was walking over to check on where he went. I tossed it right before I came in."

"And why would you do that?"

"I thought the front desk guy might have a gun. And if I came in here waving a knife, I might get shot."

It's a good answer, and I can tell by the expression on her face and the fact that she's at a momentary loss for words that she thinks so, too.

"Why didn't you tell me this earlier?"

"I guess it slipped my mind in all the commotion."

"Right."

Now she looks suspicious, and I can't say I blame her. It didn't slip my mind. It just took me a while to come up with a good excuse for ditching it. "Let's go over to the unit. I need you to identify that toothbrush for us."

"Where did you find blood?" I ask.

"I can't comment on an ongoing investigation."

I swallow. That sounds like something you'd say to a suspect.

Wait until they find out about the two-million-dollar life insurance policy.

HOURS HAVE PASSED, and I'm still sitting in the lobby of the resort. They only let me into the unit for a few minutes to identify Kyle's toothbrush, and then Martinez escorted me back here, informing me that the room is now a crime scene, along with the resort. An officer is posted outside the door, and I feel like a prisoner. I wonder if I should call an attorney.

I have no idea where the front desk guy is. Timmy's his name, which I found amusing. A diminutive name on such a large, lumbering man. He doesn't look like a Timmy. More like a Harold or a Walter. And I wonder if this is a normal thought to have at a time like this, or if I'm losing it.

I'm trying to stay calm, but I'm dying to text Carla. I don't dare, though. They might ask to see my phone. But we need to talk. Soon. I'm sure if they drive by and see the place swarming with cops, they'll abort our plan.

But then you never know.

Perhaps one of them decided to kidnap Kyle for real. Hold him for ransom. Could this be my fault? Could Kyle be in danger because of me? I'm starting to think this was a terrible idea, and I'm overcome with fear at the thought of where he might be now. It's one thing for him to be looking at me as he takes his last breath. I'd make it painless. But I don't want him to suffer.

And I'm not even sure what I would have done if he'd admitted he was cheating. All I wanted was to tie him to a chair, look him in the eye, and get the truth out of him. And to watch him squirm a little.

Is that asking too much?

Officer Martinez comes into the lobby with Timmy. "We got surveillance video of the attack," she says.

My eyes widen. This is great news for me. At least they'll believe me now.

"We'd like you to take a look. See if you recognize the man."

"Of course," I say.

They take me into a back room, and I watch what plays on the screen—a dark and empty pathway in front of the beach. It's surreal seeing the event play out, this time with me as an observer. I come into the frame, walking with the knife in my fist.

Good thing I came clean about that.

He comes out of nowhere, into the camera's view, and

reality hits me like a gut punch as I watch it, nearly crumbling as I take it all in. My reaction time is impressive. Those self-defense classes certainly paid off. But I'm not feeling victorious, and I have to fight the wave of emotion that's nearly causing me to break down and cry.

The officer puts her hand on mine, and I steel myself. Although I'm trying to hide it, I'm visibly shaken.

"I know things like this can be traumatic," she says. "I'm going to play it one more time. Is that okay?"

I nod, but that's not what's bothering me.

I'm not traumatized, I'm crushed.

After the second time, I'm sure of what I'm seeing, and my world comes crashing down.

"Do you recognize him?" she asks.

I shake my head no.

But that's a lie.

I'd know that gait anywhere.

It's Kyle on the tape.

Kyle tried to kill me.

NINE

TARA

Finally! A story that's worth my getting out of bed in the morning. I bolt out of my chair and race into my station manager's office.

"You have to let me go!" I say.

"Go where?" Brett Cavanaugh asks.

"To Saratoga. To cover the Murphy case."

"That's not your primary responsibility anymore, Tara. You're a weekend anchor now."

"Anchor, schmanker. Come on! You owe me." I stand my ground like a toddler demanding an ice cream cone before dinner. This probably isn't the best approach. But he knows me pretty well, and I think I can get away with it.

"I owe you?" He leans back in his chair and eyes me, letting me know I'm pushing it here, but I press on.

I throw up my hands. "I covered a pet parade, for Christ's sake. Just let me have it, Brett. I promise I'll get an exclusive with the wife."

He rolls his eyes. "That's an impossible thing to promise, Tara, and you know it."

"If anyone can do it, I can. And *you* know it. Who were you planning to send? Before I so generously offered my services?" I smirk.

"Neil."

My hands fly to my hips. "Neil? You can't send a man. This is a delicate situation, requiring a woman's touch."

"You're about as delicate as a land shark, Tara."

I roll my eyes. "You know what I mean."

This approach isn't working.

I switch gears.

"Please?" I pout and drag out my plea like it's my dying wish. "Think about how great it will be when I get the scoop. I'll give you all the credit. Tell them it was all your idea to send me. Delicate little me." I drape my hands down the sides of my body. Then I put on my best *I'll be a good girl from now on* face.

He lets out a sigh, and I know I've won.

"You won't be sorry," I say.

I rush out to get my team assembled.

This isn't about ego. Well, maybe a little it is, but not totally. I wanted to be a journalist to cover hard news. To make a difference in the world. And frankly, I've been a trifle bored as of late. This case promises to be the most exciting news story in years, and I thrive on the thrill of it.

But it's also because I covered the last sensational missing persons case in the Bay Area, nearly a decade ago, when I was just starting out. My coverage won an award, and I captivated the public. But I made mistakes. I didn't trust my gut, and I let the frenzy steer me instead of the other way around. I was too insecure at the time. I have some serious regrets about that, because there were consequences. This time, I'm steering the narrative.

This time, I'm getting it right.

TEN

MORGAN

I didn't want to believe it. Part of me had been hoping that I was wrong about Kyle, like Carla had been about Eddie. That there was some explanation that would be obvious in hindsight. We'd have a good laugh about it and he'd call me his little minx and we'd launch into steamy hot make-up sex.

But now it's clear to me what happened, and I've never felt so alone. I got home about two in the morning, and I barely slept last night. Carla came to get me. They agreed to let me call her, around eleven o'clock, and luckily, she caught my drift. I sounded hysterical when I phoned her, and it wasn't an act. I told Carla that Kyle was missing. And that someone also tried to kidnap me, too, and I needed her to come right away.

Our plan didn't involve anything having to do with me, so that tipped her off to the fact that something had gone very wrong. Plus, Eddie's guys were supposed to "break in" through the sliding door, which I left open, and grab Kyle in the middle of the night, not at nine o'clock, and take him to a warehouse in Sunnyvale. Carla's not stupid, and she played the part of frantic best friend to a tee.

When we got in the car, I finally broke down and cried. I could barely get the story out. But once I did, Carla tried her best to console me.

"Are you sure it was Kyle?" she asked. "How could you tell? Those videos aren't very high quality, and you didn't see his face."

"It was him, Carla."

"But you didn't have any sense of it when he grabbed you. Don't you think you would have picked up on it? Recognized his scent? Or his breathing?"

At the time, I dismissed her observations. But I have to admit, I am thinking about it now, especially with my keen sense of smell. But there was something rotting out on that beach, and the scent was overpowering. And then the attacker had that cloth on my face. Still, Carla has a point. Maybe I'm wrong and it wasn't Kyle on the tape. I suppose I'll have to wait and see if it was his blood they found.

But if it wasn't Kyle on the tape, then what the hell is going on?

Who would take him?

The police followed us to my house and asked if they could come inside. I said yes, although I know it was my right to refuse. They asked if they could take Kyle's computer, and I gave it to them. They asked to wiretap my phone, in case a ransom call came in. I obliged. Then they requested my computer, and that's where I drew the line. I said I'd consult with an attorney and mumbled something about a warrant and needing to sleep. And they left.

Another thought crossed my mind this morning. What if

one of Eddie's guys decided to go rogue? Kidnap both of us? But if they wanted ransom, then how would they get it if they were holding both of us?

That doesn't make sense.

Plus, Carla will have a fit if I asked her about it, and I don't want to alienate her.

Meanwhile, I'm terrified about what this means for Kyle's stalled project. I need to find out more about Wes Walker. If Kyle's missing, Walker's money will be tied up, and he's not going to like that. But then a thought crosses my mind.

The life insurance.

Two million dollars.

If there's no body, I bet it takes forever to get paid out. I want to do an internet search about that, but I don't dare. I'm clearly a person of interest. They always investigate the spouse. And if I become a suspect and they get that warrant, they'll take my computer and see what I've been up to.

It helps my case that someone tried to take me, too. We are the beneficiaries of each other's policies. So, if someone took the two of us, there would be nobody to collect the insurance money. But still, they might think we planned something together. Faked Kyle's disappearance to collect the life insurance.

If only.

My stomach sinks as I realize how alone I am, with no real family besides Kyle. It's Sunday, and I'm itching to go to work. At work, I have access to information. Here, I feel useless, and I don't know how I'll get through the day. The sun is just starting to rise, and I can see rays of light peeking in through the curtains in front of our plate glass window as I sit on the sofa, sipping my coffee, staring into space.

How will I pass the time?

I make my way over to the living room window to open the curtains and let some light in, thinking that it might pull me out of my stupor. I start to pull them open, and my eyes nearly pop out of my head. Three vans sit in front of our townhouse, waiting to pounce.

The media.

Of course.

This is going to be one of those high-profile missing persons cases. The kind that goes viral with true crime fanatics and talk show hosts and conspiracy theorists clamoring for the inside scoop—a total disaster.

What if one of Eddie's guys decides to sell his story to the tabloids? If they find out what I was planning that night, they'll think I did something to Kyle.

And suddenly, I'm snapped out of my depressed state over the failure of my marriage and infused with a dose of self-preservation instinct that gets my adrenaline flowing.

I need a new plan.

And an attorney.

And I need to craft a believable persona for the press, and use it to my advantage.

One point in my favor is with the media camped outside my home, it will be harder for Wes Walker or whoever's after us to get to me. But that won't last forever. I need a plan to save myself.

And I need it now.

ELEVEN
MORGAN

Rather than hide myself away, I decide that the best strategy is to be as visible as possible and work with the press. I did some acting as a teenager, and I was good at it. So good, I got the lead in *Romeo and Juliet* when I was only a junior, and it pissed off a popular senior girl who thought she was a shoo-in.

I may have been mousy, but I was a romantic at heart, and the thought of loving someone so much that you'd rather die than live without them is a feeling I yearned for. My performance brought down the house. The real tragedy of that play is not so much that they died, but that they died one at a time, not together. Bonnie and Clyde. Now there's a couple who knew how to make an exit.

What does one wear for their first run-in with the press? Something not too sexy, but not too dowdy either. Not black. That will seem like I've given up. Nothing too bright, though. My clothes are strewn all over the bedroom, and I've landed on the perfect outfit. A baby blue long-sleeved sweater dress that sits just above the knee, low-heeled black strappy sandals, and the diamond heart necklace Kyle got me for our tenth anniversary. I put all the clothes away, in case the police decide to ransack my house.

My make-up is minimal, and I've used waterproof mascara, so that when I cry, it won't run down my face. I'm sure the police would rather coach me before I talk to anyone, but I have no idea how much they know or what they're up to. I'm expecting that at some point they'll come with a warrant and search the house. In fact, I'm surprised that they left last night. But I'm not waiting for them. They might even arrest me. This might be my only chance to shape public opinion.

It's just after eight in the morning. I take a deep breath, open the front door, and walk outside. There are five vans now, and it takes a few minutes for the reporters to get out and start towards me. I stand with my arms folded, rubbing my upper arms with my hands. It's chilly, colder than it seemed from inside the house.

There're two men and three women. I recognize one of them, a popular local reporter and weekend anchor, Tara Harker from K-PAL, our leading TV news station. I'm surprised and delighted by the fact that she's come. I make eye contact with her and offer her a nervous smile.

"Ms. Murphy," she says, cutting in front of the other reporters.

I like that.

She puts a hand on my arm. "How are you?"

"Cold," I say, barely above a whisper. "And tired."

"Well," she says, cocking her head to one side. "If you

want to give me an exclusive, we could do this inside. In a more...comfortable setting."

I try to appear hesitant, but I'm thrilled by her offer. After a few moments, I respond. "Yes." I nod. "But I want some time to talk to you before the cameras roll."

"That's a deal," she says.

Grabbing her camera guy, she opens the door to my home, and I follow her in. "Shut it off, Billy," she says. "Go into the kitchen and give us some privacy, please."

He complies.

We sit on the sofa, a respectable distance apart.

"Do you want to tell me what happened?" she asks.

I run her through the basics, and her eyes widen when I tell her that I fought the guy off.

"That's impressive," she says.

"I've taken some classes."

"Wise move," she says. "More women should do that. You're a great role model."

She flips her silky dark hair off her shoulder. I shrug, not sure how to take her compliment. She seems to be kissing up to me a bit too much, and I know reporters can be manipulative. I'm on guard now, but I don't let on about it. Continuing with the rest of my story, I get to the part about finding the blood.

"And you don't know where they found it or if it's your husband Kyle's blood?"

"Right. The police don't seem to want to tell me much."

We discuss the various ways we could do the interview, and we land on a plan. She calls her camera guy back in. Before we start, she takes out a compact, touches up her bright pink lipstick, and powders her face. She's attractive and poised, a few years older than me, and she gives off a friendly vibe on air. But the intense look on her face before she starts clues me into the fact that she's a serious journalist, and this isn't going to be a fluff piece. I hope I haven't made a mistake.

"We're here in Saratoga, California, in the living room of Morgan and Kyle Murphy. Last night, at a beach resort on the coast near Monterey Bay, Ms. Murphy was attacked and nearly kidnapped, and her husband, Kyle Murphy, is now missing."

She feeds me the questions we discussed, and I answer them, keeping a shaky timbre in my voice and a timid, vulnerable expression on my face. I explain how I was grabbed from behind, what the man was wearing, and how I managed to get away.

"Wow, you're a regular *Charlie's Angel*," she says. "Take note, all you women out there. Self-defense classes really pay off, and Morgan Murphy is living proof of that."

I offer her a humble shrug. "I got lucky," I say. "It could have gone another way."

"Ms. Murphy's just being modest."

She asks me about Kyle, and about our marriage. I start to choke up, and it's not an act. We were a happy couple, I tell her. We've been together for ten years. Inseparable. I struggle to compose myself as a wave of emotion comes over me.

"Cut the camera, Billy," she says.

She waits for me to cry it out, patting me on the back. After a few minutes, we roll again. I go over the fact that he's missing. The blood they found. And that we don't know yet if it was Kyle's.

"Anything else you'd like to say before we wrap up?" Tara asks.

"This was supposed to be a little romantic getaway, to spice up our relationship. And now Kyle's gone, and all I want is for him to come back to me. Please, if you are holding my husband, I'll give you anything. Tell me what you want. But don't hurt Kyle. He's all I have."

I take a deep breath, eager to wrap it up. It went well, and I don't want to push it.

But Tara's brow is furrowed, and there's an intense look on her face. "Wait. Morgan?" she says. "I'm a little confused. Why did you need to spice up your marriage if you were such a happy couple? Were you and Kyle having marital problems?"

My stomach lurches, and I feel my nostrils flare.

What the hell kind of question was that?

I'm fuming, but I soften my expression. I can't appear aggressive or defensive. The public needs to feel sympathy for me.

"I didn't mean anything by that, Tara. Everyone likes a little variety, now and then. There was nothing wrong with my marriage."

"Well, thanks for clearing that up, Morgan. This is Tara Harker, bringing you the exclusive on the disappearance of real estate developer Kyle Murphy."

Once the cameras are off, I glare at her. "Why did you ask me that question?"

"I'm a journalist, Morgan. Not your PR agent. And this is just getting started. If I were you, I'd get some help on this. The court of public opinion is brutal, even more so than a criminal court, and that was a stupid thing to say on air. You seem like a bright woman, and you might think you can outsmart everyone. But a situation like this is out of your league. I'm not out to destroy you, but I have an obligation to get at the truth. It's all going to come out sooner or later, so if there's something you want to get off your chest and you want to talk again, here's my card."

She hands it to me and they get up and leave.

"When will this air?" I ask.

"The noon broadcast, but it will start streaming before then. Probably in an hour or two."

I nod. "I trust you can see yourselves out," I say.

"Of course. Keep in touch, Morgan," she says. "I'm not the worst of the pack."

For some reason, I believe her.

And I have a feeling that my world is about to come crashing down around me.

TWELVE
MORGAN

I've resisted the urge to glue myself to the K-PAL website and busied myself cleaning the house. It's an odd quirk of mine. Cleaning relaxes me, and I've been accused of being a neat freak. It's almost noon, and I'm waiting for the broadcast to come on.

I can only hope that the camera spared me when my face turned severe. Kyle jokes with me that I have an angry resting face. He claims that when I'm deep in concentration, I look like I want to kill your whole family. He's constantly reminding me to smile, especially when we're meeting new people. That only serves to make me grin like a psychotic, homicidal clown, which is even worse. What does my face look like when I'm furious?

I shudder to think.

The broadcast starts, and there's Tara Harker on my big screen TV, poised and coiffed, aside her co-anchor Doug Raymond. They could be brother and sister. She starts, and my stomach sinks when I realize that I'm the lead story. But then, what did I expect?

"We're bringing you an exclusive interview with Morgan Murphy in her Saratoga home. Ms. Murphy narrowly escaped a potentially brutal attack last night at Crescent Cove Resort just outside Monterey Bay. Her husband, Kyle Murphy, is now missing."

They cut to my living room, and so far, so good. The first time the camera pans me, I've got a strained smile on my face. A grin-and-bear-it kind of look that matches the occasion. I come across as nervous, which is only natural. The interview starts, and I try to stay neutral as I view myself on the screen.

What would I think if I'd never heard of Kyle and Morgan Murphy?

It comes off well when I brush off Tara's compliment about my self-defense moves, but I wonder what people will think about the fact that I can fight off a man. It might make me less sympathetic. The part where I break down and cry comes off as authentic. I get choked up again, just watching myself, so I'm sure it resonated with the audience.

But then comes my appeal.

And my blunder.

I want to smack myself.

What was I thinking?

I hold my breath, hoping that the camera spares me. But of course, it doesn't. As soon as Tara asks me that question about marital problems, the camera cuts to me.

In an instant, I'm transformed from grieving wife to murderous maniac. Flared nostrils. Tight jaw. My normally clear blue eyes streaked red from crying. In short, I'm hideous. The menacing expression is fleeting. I catch myself and force my face into a softer look. But it's obvious that I'm faking it.

This is a disaster.

Tara wraps up the interview and cuts back to the station.

My phone buzzes. It's Carla, and I let it go to voicemail. She's probably freaking out, thinking that someone will figure out what we were planning. But I can't deal with her now.

"In more breaking news, we've just found out that the blood found on the scene belonged to Kyle Murphy. More to come as the story develops."

My stomach sinks.

It's Kyle's blood?

Nothing makes sense to me now. If Kyle was taken by someone, then it wasn't him on the security tape. Which means that either one of Eddie's guys took him, or Wes Walker or some other enemy of Kyle's struck first. I need to talk to Carla in person. I text her, instructing her to come around the back of the complex. There's a walking path, and she can enter through the back patio and avoid the media.

She replies immediately.

I'll be there inside of an hour.

CARLA KNOCKS on the back door, right on schedule. And I can tell by the look on her face that her debt to me has been fully paid—and then some. All I did was get them some free legal advice when Eddie owed money to the IRS, so I can't say I blame her. It saved them a ton of money, but she never put me in legal jeopardy.

"What the hell is going on?" she asks.

"I don't know, Carla. Kyle's missing. It's his blood. Someone must have taken him. Are you sure it wasn't one of Eddie's guys?"

"Are you crazy? They thought it was a prank. Like we told them. A spicy role-playing thing. Remember? It was your idea to keep the truth from them, and thank goodness we did. You think they would go in for an actual kidnapping for a few hundred dollars? Don't you be turning this on me, Morgan. If this goes south, I'm just as screwed as you are."

"I'm sorry, Carla. I know. It was a stupid idea. I didn't want to kill him. I just wanted to scare the shit out of him and look him in the eye. Get him to come clean with me. And now he's gone. *For real.* If what we were planning comes out, nobody will believe that I had nothing to do with this."

"I did some damage control with the guys," Carla says. "I told them that Kyle was in some financial trouble, and that you're fearing they'll come after you. You were assaulted, so that's a point in your favor. Hopefully, they'll keep their mouths shut. But with this story going viral—"

"Viral?" My stomach sinks.

"Haven't you been online?"

I take a deep breath. "I've been avoiding it. Is it that bad?"

"Is it that bad? It's everywhere. That picture of your face, looking like you want to murder Tara Harker. Memes. Posts on every social media platform. I wouldn't be surprised if you're the opening skit on *Saturday Night Live* this week."

Shit! Shit!

Me and my damn angry resting face.

"What should I do, Carla? Do you think one of Eddie's guys will talk?"

"I don't know. I mean, if someone from the press offers them money. Or if there's some kind of reward, then they might. Unless you want to offer them something first?"

"Are you crazy? I'm a paralegal. That's witness tampering. Right now, I've done nothing but engineer a fun, sexy prank. *Try* to engineer a fun, sexy prank. It didn't even happen."

Then I get an idea.

I don't dare share it with Carla.

Because it's insane.

But it just might be my only move.

I need to move fast.

I make up an excuse, telling Carla that I need to meet with an attorney and that she should get going. Which isn't a lie. I've already called Roger, the one who looks like a giant baby. He's surprisingly effective in criminal cases, and I can trust him. He'll be over in a few hours.

But before he comes, I'm going to act on my instincts. I see Carla out the back gate. Then I pull out the card from Tara Harker and punch in her number.

"Tara Harker." She picks up almost immediately.

"Tara? It's Morgan Murphy," I say. "I have an exclusive for you. When can you come over?"

"How's now?" she says.

"Now is perfect."

It's time to face the music. I flip open my laptop and do a search for my name. And it's even worse than I thought. My face is distorted into an angry grimace. Not only do I look maniacal, I'm also unattractive.

Wonderful!

Morgan the Maniac is actually trending.

I check some missing persons websites, and Kyle's case is the first one that pops up on two of the three. I click on one of the sites and take a look at the comments. My throat feels like it's about to close up.

She's guilty.

Did you see her face?

OMG Tara Harker's next.

Calm down, everyone.

But someone tried to kill her.

I slam the computer down, head into the kitchen, and get a drink of water. Then I sit, staring into space, trying to make sense of it all. If it wasn't Kyle on the tape, who was it? Where is Kyle now? Who was the woman he was meeting with? Is someone going to come after me? Who's more of a threat to me? The police—or the guy who tried to grab me? And shouldn't the police be offering me some kind of protection?

After ten minutes or so, there's a knock at my door.

That was fast.

A wave of panic shoots through me, and I have second thoughts about what I'm planning to divulge to Tara Harker.

But it can't get any worse than this.

Can it?

THIRTEEN
MORGAN

It's just after noon, and the media have multiplied. I watch as Tara Harker and her camera guy make their way through the growing crowd in front of my townhouse.

"I need him to wait out here," I say to her. "I want to talk with you in private."

"Billy, wait in the van," Tara snips.

We head in and get seated in my living room. With the drapes closed, it seems dark and depressing, so I put on a few more lights. Tara sits on the lounger. I take the sofa, kitty corner to her.

She smiles, leans in, and places her hand on my arm. "I'm glad you called me, Morgan. I want to help."

That's bullshit, but I smile back. We both know this is all for show. She wants a scoop and I want to get ahead of this public relations nightmare.

We deserve each other.

"So why am I here?" she asks.

"I wanted to answer your question," I say. "But first, I

need you to know that I have no idea where my husband is, and I had nothing to do with his disappearance. That's the God's honest truth."

"I believe you," she says, with conviction. "But again, Morgan. Why am I here?"

"What I'm going to tell you is very personal. I'm nervous about it. It's not something I want to share with the world. But with this story going viral, it will all come out. And I think it's better if it comes from me."

She sits back and folds her arms. "Okay. You've got me now, Morgan."

I swallow.

"Take your time," she says.

I take a deep breath and start. "In our last interview, I said that we went on this little getaway to spice things up. And then you asked me if we were having marital problems."

"Yes."

"But that's not what I meant when I said I wanted to spice things up. Nothing was wrong. But you see, Kyle and I have a very...hot, steamy relationship." I feel my face flush a little but I keep going. "And we like it that way. We've been married for ten years, and we've been able to sustain the tension and excitement by keeping each other on our toes."

Her eyes widen, and I can tell this isn't at all what she was expecting. But she can't hide her exuberance. Judging from the way her mouth curves up at the corners, it's clear that this is the right move.

I continue. "We role-play sometimes. You know, prisoner and warden. Housewife and pool boy. That kind of thing. And we like to mix it up. Have sex in public places. Airplane stalls. Restaurant bathrooms." I smile. "Kyle calls me his little minx."

She nods, and I swear I see her blush, but she's still got a look of salacious delight on her face.

"I know it might sound strange, but our love for each other is intense, and it gets hotter as the years go on. So many couples struggle with this. How to keep the fires burning. Divorce rates are through the roof. I wasn't going to let that happen to us. Our love affair is one for the ages, and we both want to keep it like that."

"Okay. But what does this have to do with what happened last night?"

"When he told me about this romantic anniversary getaway, I decided to take it up a notch. And this time, I hired some guys to 'kidnap' him"—my fingers fly up into air quotes—"and take him to a warehouse in Sunnyvale. It was supposed to be a prank. A fun, sexy prank that never even happened. It was scheduled to go down later in the evening. They weren't supposed to take me. So, when someone grabbed me, I knew it had gone terribly wrong. And now Kyle's gone. The police found his blood. I have no idea where he is or what's happening to him. That's the truth, I swear it."

Her eyes nearly pop out of her head. "Do you think these people you hired decided to act on their own and take him for real?"

"No. I know they didn't. I called it off when he went missing. This is something different. I can feel it. Kyle was in some financial trouble. Maybe it has something to do with that. There's money missing from our bank accounts, and one of his development projects has stalled."

"And there've been no ransom demands?"

"No. Nothing."

"Did you tell the police all of this?" she asks.

"Not yet," I say. "Because I didn't think they'd believe me. I've seen the stories of victims turned into suspects. Remember that couple from the East Bay? The police thought they'd faked their own home invasion, and nobody would believe the woman was kidnapped and sexually assaulted."

"I remember, yes. It nearly ruined their lives."

"And she was telling the truth the whole time. The police got tunnel vision, and that guy assaulted other women. What are the chances the police will believe me? I want an opportunity to tell the public my side of the story, before the police get wind of it and twist this into something it's not."

"You've come to the right person," she assures me. "Now let's get rolling before any of this comes out."

"YOU DID WHAT?" Roger leaps up from the sofa, his head in his hands. "Morgan, are you crazy? When is it going to air?"

"On the five o'clock evening news."

"Good grief. What were you thinking?"

"I was thinking that the court of public opinion is tougher than a criminal court, and I wanted to get ahead of this."

"And you think this is the way to do it? Broadcast the

details of your sex life on network TV? Tell everyone you were planning to *fake kidnap* your husband?"

"I had nothing to do with what happened to Kyle," I assure him. "They won't find any evidence of that, because there's nothing to find."

"You sure about that?" he asks.

"What are you implying, Roger?"

He waves his hands in the air, attempting to brush off his comment. "Nothing, Morgan. I believe you. That's not what I meant. I'm sure you think there's no evidence. But you never know what they'll find and how it will come off to the police. What if someone's trying to frame you?"

My stomach lurches.

I hadn't thought of that.

The only person who knows what I was up to is Carla, and she's got no motive.

"To what end?"

"Who knows. Tell me more about the financial problems." Roger already informed me that the Santa Clara County police are collaborating with the Monterrey officers, running a joint investigation, and he's sure that means that more information has surfaced.

I explain a bit more about the stalled development project and the zoning issues. My concerns about Wes Walker. The rumors I heard years ago about him and the illegal timber importing business.

"So that's why you were digging around in the criminal databases last week? And why you ducked out for a few long lunches for some *medical problem?*"

"You knew about that?" I ask.

He shrugs. "I wasn't born under a rock yesterday, Morgan."

I shake my head and smile, in spite of the gravity of the situation.

"Illegal timber importing. Where did you hear that about Walker?" he asks.

"At my last firm. One of the partners there knew something about it," I say. "He was a client of ours, around the time that Lumber Liquidators case broke. I didn't know the details. Only that he came in for a consultation around that time. He's been Kyle's supplier for years. And he's invested about a million in this new project."

"You think Kyle was mixed up in it? Like he was helping him launder money or something?"

"No. That's not what I meant. Just that he didn't seem like the kind of guy who would take it well if his investment evaporated."

"Why would he harm Kyle?" he says. "Seems like Kyle would be worth more to him alive than dead."

My stomach sinks. "Well..." I fiddle with my necklace and stare off into space, biting my lip. "As of last week, that's not quite true."

"What are you trying to tell me?" Roger asks.

"Kyle took out a two-million-dollar life insurance policy. On both of us." I wince a little as the words leave my lips.

Roger sits on the sofa, holding his head in his hands, staring down at the hardwood floor. Then he glares at me with widened eyes. "Morgan. When this comes out, you're fucked. You know how this will look?"

I don't dare tell him about my cheating suspicions, and I

can only hope that Carla keeps her mouth shut about that. If I tell him, he'll see right through my sexy prank ruse.

"Someone tried to kidnap me," I remind him.

Because it's true.

And I need to keep the focus on that.

"I hate to say this, Morgan. But have you considered the possibility that Kyle set that up? To collect the insurance money and pay off his debt after he got rid of you? You said the getaway was his idea. Maybe they decided to kill him instead. If they did, you'll probably get a ransom demand."

His words hit me like a freight train. I start to shake, and my knees buckle from under me. Roger springs up to steady me and helps me to the sofa. A wave of grief overtakes me, but I steady myself. It's one thing for a thought like that to flash through my mind. But hearing it from Roger makes it real. And he doesn't even know about my cheating suspicions.

My marriage.

Our life together.

Was it all a sham?

I can't let on that I'm having doubts about that to anyone, though. I need the public, and my attorney, to believe the fantasy.

Morgan and Kyle.

A romance for the ages.

In the meantime, I need a strategy to keep myself out of prison. After a few minutes, I straighten up and brush myself off. I assure him that it's not possible, that Kyle would never betray me. He apologizes. Roger and I work out a plan, starting with him making an appointment for us to talk to the police first thing tomorrow morning. We go over what I already told them, in detail.

"I'm actually shocked that they've stayed away this long," he says. "That doesn't really make sense. We need to reach out. Have you keep pressure on them."

I nod.

He's right. It doesn't make sense that they've been so quiet, but I don't want to think about that now. I can only hope it's not because they're collecting evidence to spring a surprise arrest on me. That's why I need to move fast. As we're wrapping things up and I'm about to see him out the door, I ask him one last question.

"Roger?"

"Yes, Morgan?"

"How long does it take to collect on life insurance if there's no body?"

"I'm not sure."

"Find out," I say.

He nods and heads out the door.

FOURTEEN
MORGAN

My heart is pounding so hard, I can hear it in my ears as I sit on the sofa, waiting for the five o'clock news to come on. So much has happened in the last twenty-four hours it's hard to believe that it's real. I'm exhausted, and I need to sleep. But I know that what's about to happen will rock my world.

I haven't told Carla about this, and she's going to flip. Roger said that nothing major can happen to Carla or the guys if they didn't actually do anything, but the police could come after them with an attempted kidnapping charge. He doesn't think it would amount to anything—unless one of them actually did take Kyle. In that case, I'd welcome the inquiry. There's been no ransom demand, though, so that's unlikely.

The news comes on. I'm not the lead story. Some kind of campus protest starts off the broadcast, and I can't help but feel a bit insulted.

Isn't my missing husband more important?

They cut back to the anchor desk after a few minutes.

Tara Harker introduces the story and cuts to the interview. I seem nervous, which is good. Anyone would be nervous in this situation. My eyes are puffy, but I'm presentable.

"So why are we here?" Tara asks. "What is it you want people to know?"

I hesitate. "This is hard," I say. "What I'm about to say is highly personal."

"Take your time, Morgan." Tara pats my hand.

I swallow and take a deep breath.

And then it all starts rolling off my tongue. My description of our steamy hot marriage. How we've been able to keep the fires of passion going, even after ten years. How he calls me his little minx.

"What does this have to do with Kyle's kidnapping?"

This is the tricky part. But watching myself, I'm delighted with how it's coming off. I explain to the viewers about my fun, sexy prank and how I was going to fake kidnap Kyle. I tell them that the guys were instructed to let Kyle know it was a gag, which is true.

I become emotional when I get to the part about my husband being missing for real, and it's not an act. I'm truly conflicted. One minute hating him for possibly cheating; missing him desperately the next. Explaining how I was grabbed and almost kidnapped myself, I have to take a moment because I start to tremble and my voice cracks. I assure the viewers that this was not our little gag gone bad, and it looks believable.

"And there's been no ransom demand?"

"No. None."

"It seems a bit of a coincidence that you were planning this stunt and then something actually happened to him,"

Tara offers. "Do you think someone decided to change the plan? Maybe one of the people you hired?"

"No. That's not possible. They'd have nothing to gain from that."

"Does Kyle have any enemies?" she asks.

I take a deep breath, knowing that I'm threading a needle here. I need to plant a seed for the public, but stop short of implicating someone like Wes Walker. "I'm not sure. We've been having some financial trouble. One of his development projects has stalled. But I don't see what killing him would do to fix that."

"The police mentioned they found blood at the scene. And it's been determined that it's Kyle's blood."

My face goes pale. I rest my head in my hands. Tara rubs my back. After a minute or so, I sit up, look into the camera, and speak earnestly.

"Something terrible happened to my husband. And the longer this goes on without a ransom demand, the worse the prospects are of finding him. Someone must have seen something. If anyone has any information about what happened, please call the police."

And then we're out.

Perfect.

THE REAL TEST comes about an hour later, which is the amount of time I forced myself to wait until I started combing through social media. I flip open my laptop and start searching.

Morgan the Minx is trending.

Better than *Morgan the Maniac.*

I head back over to the true crime site where I saw the comments earlier. They've mushroomed, and most of the posts seem to be on my side.

So who took Kyle Murphy?
I heard he's kinda shady.
Crazy story, right?
She's got nothing to gain by telling that story.
She's annoying, but I believe her.

For the most part, it's playing out the way I imagined because people are asking themselves exactly what I was hoping they'd ask. Why would I go on air and admit to engineering a fake kidnapping prank if I'd murdered my husband?

It's the perfect defense, especially because I know there's no evidence that I took him. Even if the police come after me and get enough for an indictment, which I doubt, they'll never get a jury to believe that I'd be stupid enough to tell the world about my prank when I'd actually killed my husband.

Except there's one person who can screw up my plan.

Carla.

And she has a bad temper.

I had my phone turned off for the interview, so I power it up. There are five text messages and two voicemails from her. She's furious, I can tell. But she's holding back, not saying anything incriminating, just imploring me to call her. The last one sends chills up my spine and it's clear that I need to do some damage control.

Should I give Tara Harker a call?

I'm sure she'd like another scoop.

I call Roger first and tell him that Carla wants to come to the station with us tomorrow to back me up. He agrees that it will strengthen my case, and now I need to get her on board. I text her, asking if she can meet me at the house, and tell Roger to meet us here. She responds immediately.

I'll be there in fifteen minutes.

Don't go anywhere.

Heading over to my social media accounts, I comb through to see how this is playing out in my inner circle. Mostly there are supportive posts from friends and acquaintances, with a few hot chili pepper emojis that make me blush. Kyle and I are a private couple, and it's a little embarrassing to share the details of my sex life with the world. If it'll keep me out of prison, though, it's worth it.

But then I notice that I've got a slew of friend requests from total strangers. And a bunch of DMs. I take a deep breath, expecting death threats or vulgar come-ons. Much to my shock and delight, that's not what I find when I click on the first one.

Morgan. I loved your interview, and I hope you find Kyle soon. But I really need help. My husband and I used to be like that, but our spark has fizzled. Can you give me some advice? I need to get the fire back.

Aside from one message from a woman who wants to see me burn in hell, most of the messages are like this. Cries for help from people wanting to get some spark back in their relationship. Men. Women. Gay. Straight. All searching for what I have.

What I had.

And now I have to force myself to believe in my own fairy tale. Kyle didn't betray me. Someone's taken him. I'm going to convince Carla of that. And then we're going to convince the police. Because public opinion is with me now.

And I need to keep it that way.

CARLA MARCHES INTO MY KITCHEN, through the back door. "What were you thinking, going on air like that, Morgan?"

"It was the only way, Carla. You said it yourself. One of them might have talked to the press. And if it came out that way, it would have been worse."

"For you!" she says, throwing her hands in the air.

"For all of us."

"I was an idiot to get wrapped up in this in the first place," she says, shaking her head.

"I'm sorry. All I wanted was a chance to look him in the eye, Carla. To find out what was going on. You, of all people, should understand that."

"What's that supposed to mean?"

"What? Nothing. I'm just saying you were in a similar circumstance."

"I was never in a similar circumstance. I have no idea what you're talking about." She widens her eyes.

That's an odd thing to say.

"This was a prank. A silly prank that never even had a chance to happen. I have no idea where Kyle is."

"If you do, Morgan, you can tell me. Maybe I can help you figure a way out of this."

WTF? Is she wearing a wire or something?

"Carla! Someone tried to kidnap me. Kill me. Remember?"

"Right. I know. Sorry, Morgan. I just wish you would have given me a heads-up about that interview."

"Can we sit? And figure out what to do from here? Can I get you anything?"

She shakes her head no and sits at my island countertop, resting her forearms on its light granite surface. "So, what's our plan? We're going to the police tomorrow to tell them what you just broadcast to the world? With this Roger guy from your firm?"

"Yes."

"And it won't cost me anything?"

"It won't cost you a dime," I say.

Thankfully, this awkward conversation ends when the doorbell rings. It's probably Roger. But something's up with Carla.

Have the police gotten to her?

Roger said it was odd that they'd been so quiet. That could be the reason. They were hoping they could put a wire on Carla and get me to confess.

If they got to her, I can't say I blame her for trying to save herself. But I need to tread carefully. I'll keep my mouth shut and deny everything. The burden of proof is on the prosecution, and they've got nothing.

Hopefully.

Unless Roger's right, and someone's trying to frame me.

But who would do something like that?

And why?

I invite Roger in. The three of us get seated and we run through our strategy. Carla and I will tell them about the prank. She'll back me up. Hopefully, Carla realizes that this is in her best interest, too. She and I are the only people who know that I had suspicions about Kyle cheating on me with the brunette woman. The only two people who know that the kidnapping wasn't a prank. She'd be complicit in my plan if the truth came out.

Keeping her mouth shut protects both of us, but I don't want to say that out loud, because I'm afraid she's wearing a wire. And although you're not supposed to withhold anything from your attorney, I can't risk telling Roger that Kyle might have been cheating, even if I didn't have suspicions about Carla. I need him to believe in me.

I realize now that it was a rash move, going public about it. What if they ask us to take a lie detector test? Even I don't know what I would have done, once I had him where I wanted him. I don't even own a gun. I'm not sure I could have harmed him. So, I try to convince myself that it was a harmless prank, thinking that if I can convince myself of it, I'll be able to fake out the machine, if it comes to that.

"We need to focus the police on Kyle's financial problems," Roger says. "Carla, have you been able to find out anything more?"

"No." Carla shakes her head. "The project that got him in trouble was a side deal. The firm wasn't involved."

"And Morgan. You have a list of Kyle's investors?" Roger asks.

I do, but now I'm having second thoughts. If this Wes Walker guy is as dangerous as I think he is, I'd rather figure out a way to get him his money back. I don't need him as an enemy. But the police will find out anyway, so I suppose it will come out eventually.

"Yes," I say. And I hand him a printout of the investors and the value of their investments. We wrap things up and I see them to the front door.

"Okay, ladies. I'll meet you at the Santa Clara County police station. Eight in the morning."

Carla mouths something to me as she walks out of the door after Roger.

I've got you. Don't worry.

FIFTEEN

TARA

"What in the world?" Brett Cavanaugh, my station manager, looks at me like I'm a fine racehorse who's just pulled off a longshot win. "That was freaking awesome, Tara. Come here, you."

I walk over, and he pats me on the back. I feel like neighing, but I don't. "Just doing my job," I say.

"I just watched the raw footage. Our numbers are gonna go through the roof tonight. How did you get her to go on air with that?"

"I'll never tell," I say, and I head into my office. Nobody needs to know that the woman was dumb enough to call me up and hand me that interview on a silver platter.

But now what?

I'm a serious journalist, not a talk show host, and we've still got a missing person to find. But I'm a weekend news anchor now, and I don't have as much time as I once did for investigative reporting. It's no longer my job to dig into the story. My job is to smile for the camera and report it. But if

Morgan Murphy trusts me, and only me, I may be able to insert myself a little more than usual, and I don't mind doing some of it on my own time.

When I got this promotion five years ago, it seemed like a godsend. Great money. Prime time slot. But I miss getting my hands dirty, and this juicy story has my mouth watering. There hasn't been a Bay Area case this intriguing since the disappearance of that East Bay woman ten years ago, and it's curious to me that Morgan Murphy mentioned it.

I covered that story as a young reporter. Although in that instance, the couple was telling the truth, the Murphy case could be an elaborate deception. Could Kyle and Morgan Murphy have engineered a fake-out for some unknown reason? But it seems unlikely that Morgan Murphy would bring up that case if she and her husband were actually trying to pull off a scam. And there was a great deal of blood, unlike in the other case, indicating that Kyle Murphy might actually be dead.

My gut tells me that their marriage wasn't as spicy-hot as the wife claims, so I'm going to start there and see where it leads, beginning with Carla Flores, the friend who picked her up from the station that night. If anyone knows the truth, it's the person you call late at night when you're in the middle of a missing spouse investigation.

But first, I need to assert my dominance. Capitalize on my recent success. I head into Brett's office.

"What can I do for you, superstar?" he says.

"I want some latitude on this case," I say.

"What kind of latitude?"

"A budget, to start. And some time away from these fluff pieces you have me on."

"You hurt me, Tara. Fluff?" He's smirking, but Brett doesn't like it any more than I do—the fact that we have to spend time on feel-good stories like the local high school winning a robotics championship or a Santa Clara non-profit that rescues injured birds.

"I'll see what I can do," he says.

The station's become very bureaucratic over the last decade or so, and he's probably got to clear it with who knows how many higher-ups. In the meantime, I'll keep the momentum going, starting with Carla Flores. Most people can't resist a chance for their fifteen minutes of fame, and if she's anything like her gal pal, I'll bet she jumps on my offer.

THE EVENING BROADCAST was a smashing success, and we stayed late and popped open some champagne. But I didn't drink much of mine, because I'm anxious to dig into this case, and I need a clear head to do it. I tried to call Carla Flores, and it went to voicemail. And now I'm at my desk, transcribing my notes, trying to piece it all together. Writing it all out again helps me process what I've learned. It's quiet now. Nearly eight in the evening, with only a skeleton crew here. Peaceful, like when the whole family is sleeping, and you're the only one up, stealing a moment for yourself.

Here's what I know so far. Morgan Murphy was nearly kidnapped by a masked man at the resort. Morgan fought him off with some impressive self-defense moves. That's been confirmed by the security tape. Kyle Murphy is missing, and his blood was found at the hotel. Kyle Murphy was having some financial problems, according to his wife.

Not much to go on.

Here's what Morgan Murphy told me, information that is difficult or impossible to confirm. She and Kyle were madly in love, and into spicing up their marriage in various sexy ways. She and Carla Flores planned to fake kidnap her husband for some kind of role-playing adventure. Morgan has no idea where her husband is.

I go over my notes one more time, looking for something easy to verify. The financial problems, which I'll tackle first thing tomorrow.

So, what do I believe? What do I think? What's my gut telling me? For this part of my analysis, a little buzz can actually help, so I pour myself a fresh glass of bubbly, sit back, close my eyes, and tap into my intuitive side.

I hate when people call it "women's intuition." Everyone has access to this part of their brain, the collective wisdom stored up from years of experiences that intertwine with emotions and memories and can sometimes spark great insights. I take another sip and let it all flow together. Scenes swirl in my mind's eye. Some of it mixes with a memory from my past. Morgan reminds me of someone I knew a long time ago, and I need to be careful not to let that cloud my judgement. I'm not infallible, especially when my emotions are involved.

After a few minutes, one thought jumps out at me. I believe Morgan when she says she doesn't know where her husband is. The rest of it, I can't say. The fake kidnapping story. The perfect marriage. That could all be bullshit. But I think someone actually tried to take her that night, and I'm fairly certain she doesn't know where he is now.

Who else besides Carla Flores might have answers?

Where do I go from here?

I'm not in the frame of mind to do more research, so I turn on some tunes, sit back, and take another sip, letting the alcohol buzz envelope me. I've got nowhere else to be, and maybe I should do something about that.

But not tonight.

SIXTEEN
MORGAN

My head hurts from lack of sleep. I've been tossing and turning all night, going over this in my head again and again. It's six in the morning, and we're due at the police station in two hours. The best thing to do is not overthink it. Try to be natural.

I need something to distract me. So, rather than ruminate over what I said to Tara Harker or stress about how it might go today at the police station, I flip up my laptop and start reading the DMs asking me for relationship advice.

One woman's story jumps out at me. Sandy's her name. She tells me that she's worried her husband might be cheating on her. They've been together for five years, and he just changed jobs. She thinks he might have a crush on someone at work. He's dressing better. Watching what he eats. Going to the gym before work. This is something I can handle.

I send back a reply.

He's probably craving attention.

I move to the next one. A man tells me that he and his husband have just adopted a baby girl. And although he's thrilled, he's craving some adult alone time. But he feels guilty asking for it and doesn't want to say anything about it to his partner.

He might feel the same way. Ask him out on a date night. Never feel guilty for wanting to keep your marriage strong.

I say this from experience, because I was born to parents who were madly in love. Perhaps that's why I'm so adamant about keeping the fires burning in my own marriage. My parents were so in love, I felt sometimes that I was an interruption. And although that sounds like it was a bad thing, it wasn't. There's comfort in knowing that you're the product of a great and powerful love. My mom and dad were affectionate, but not in a creepy way. In a way that made you blush a little, but secretly long for what they had.

But then my mother fell into a deep depression. She had a miscarriage about four years after I was born, and she was never the same. I didn't know that at the time, but later my mother told me during the period when she straightened herself out. All I knew at the time was that Mommy slept a lot. And smelled weird.

That was the scotch.

She started drinking to ease the pain. Perhaps that's why I've never wanted children. I saw what losing one did to her, and I never wanted to take the chance.

I became the light of my father's life. I filled that void

and brought him joy. He died when I was seven, and my world turned on a dime once again. A massive heart attack. I'm sure it was broken heart syndrome, because although my mother was still alive, he'd lost the essence of her, and with that, the love of his life.

I was with him when it happened. We went out to breakfast every Saturday morning, leaving my mother to sleep off the booze and pills. My chocolate chip pancakes with vanilla ice cream had just arrived. Steaming hot pancakes that melted the chocolate, contrasting brilliantly with the cold ice cream. I stuffed a giant fork full into my mouth and started to chew.

My dad's eyes widened, and I thought for a minute that he was going to reprimand me, tell me to take smaller bites. But then he grabbed his chest.

"Daddy!" I cried out, knowing that something horrible was happening. I thought he was choking. "Help!" I screamed, and the diner grew silent.

His eyes locked onto mine, as if he was apologizing to me, knowing that leaving me behind was going to be a horrible fate. The rest is a blur. The waitress rushing over. Someone calling for help. A fellow patron giving him CPR. The EMTs looking somber, taking him away.

I still see my dad's eyes, reaching out to me and pulling me into him. Trying not to die, but knowing that it was too late. Leaving me an only child with a train wreck of a mother, and that wasn't even the worst of it.

I get a DM from Sandy, and I welcome the distraction.

You might be right. I've been neglecting him.

Hopping on the app, I engage with her. She confesses to me that she'd grown a little bored with her husband and had started to have eyes for other men. She'd never acted on it. But now she's regretting it, especially with the change in him. I explain the laws of attraction, and that men need to feel wanted. We land on a plan for her to buy some sexy lingerie and surprise him, reminding her to pay him a compliment now and then. She wishes me luck in finding Kyle and signs off.

And now I'm right back where I started. For a while, I almost forgot that my husband is missing and my life is exploding before my eyes. Closing my laptop, I head upstairs to get ready for my meeting. What does one wear for a visit to the police station?

Probably something comfortable.

In case they don't let me leave.

THE SMALL ROOM I'm sitting in is dingy, and the fluorescent lights overhead cast unflattering shadows on its inhabitants. They separated Carla and me at the front desk. Officer Martinez whisked her away, and Roger stayed with me. I have no idea what that means, but I don't think it's good.

We were greeted by the detective on the case who's in the room with us now. Aaron Rodman's his name. He's tall and attractive, even in this light, with smooth, dark skin and great bone structure. So far, he's been very friendly, and this is making me more nervous. I feel like they're up to something. Trying to lull me into a false sense of security so they can go in for the kill or catch me in a lie.

"That was a pretty bold move," Detective Rodman says. "Going on air with that admission."

"It's the truth," I say.

"Do you have a question for my client?" Roger asks. "We didn't come here for a critique of Mrs. Murphy's PR strategy."

Rodman smiles. A perfectly white and inviting smile, but I read a hint of mockery in it. And I can't shake the feeling that there's more to this than meets the eye. That he knows something I don't.

Did Carla already tell him what we were really up to?

Does he know something about Kyle and his dealings?

"Has anyone contacted you, Mrs. Murphy?" he asks.

"What do you mean?"

"I mean, sometimes the kidnappers make contact. With a warning not to say anything to the police. Did something like that happen? Because if it did, you need to tell us. That sort of thing never ends well."

"No," I say. "Nothing like that has happened. I'd tell you, if it did. I promise. It's not like we're super wealthy or anything. Don't those people usually want millions?"

The detective shrugs. "You never know. But if nobody's asked for ransom, we might be looking at a different scenario."

"What do you mean?" I ask.

His expression turns somber, like he's about to give me horrible news. "There's some new information, Ms. Murphy," the detective says.

My stomach sinks.

Did they find his body?

Is Kyle dead?

"What is it? Just tell me," I say.

"We've seen a few cases like this recently. Where professionals come and grab a person and hold them for a while. Carjack them. Make them empty their bank accounts. Stock accounts. Anything they can get their hands on. They usually don't kill, though. Unless someone fights back."

A whooshing sound fills my ears as my blood pressure shoots up. My heart pounds like a bass drum. "Kyle would fight back," I say, almost to myself. "You think that's what happened?"

"We're not sure. We found your husband's car."

My eyes widen. "Where?"

"At an abandoned office building in Sunnyvale." He tells me the address. "Does this location mean anything to you?"

"No," I say. "But it's closer to where he would go, if he had to get money or valuables."

And it's close to the warehouse where those guys were supposed to take Kyle.

"His body wasn't in the car. But we found more blood."

"How much blood?"

He lets out a breath. "A lot," he says. "I'm sorry, I don't have more information. We're searching the area, and we'll keep you informed. But it doesn't look good."

A wave of grief and remorse washes over me, and I feel as if I'm drowning in it. I can't catch my breath. Grabbing at my chest, I force myself to breathe. This all seemed like a fun adventure when Carla and I were planning it. A fantasy. Something that wasn't real to me. But this is as real as it gets.

"Are you okay, Morgan?" Roger asks.

I shake my head no.

"Do you need some time, Ms. Murphy?" Rodman asks.

A somber silence settles over the room as I try to compose myself. After a minute or so, I respond.

"I'm okay now. Let's keep going. I want to help. I want to catch whoever did this. There was no camera footage of him near the car?"

"No. I'm afraid your husband's car was in a blind spot. The only footage we got was your attack, which you've already seen."

"I can't believe this," I say.

And it's the truth.

I can't believe that this could be a coincidence. That we could be having financial problems. That Kyle could owe money to a shady investor. And that it could be a random hit, strangers who just happened to choose us. Why would they come to this beach resort in the middle of winter to find their targets? But at least it might deflect them from me, for the time being. I don't want to call attention to the fact that Kyle's car was found near where we were supposed to take him. That might make me look responsible. But I wonder again if one of those guys took Kyle. But then why wouldn't I have gotten a ransom demand? It doesn't make sense.

"Do you have any idea who would want to kill your husband?" the detective asks.

I shake my head no, and that's not a total lie. If it's one of his investors, why would they want him dead? And why would they be after me, too? I need some time to figure out what's happening.

And if it is Walker, I'd like to get to him before the police. If it is him, maybe he still has Kyle, and I can work out some kind of deal. Or if he had nothing to do with it, at the very least, I can assure him that he'll get his money, so he doesn't come after me.

"Kyle Murphy's been having some financial problems," Roger says. "Morgan, tell the detective what you told me."

I explain to him about the stalled project and the failed attempt at rezoning his parcel, and we hand him the list of investors. But I've instructed Roger not to mention anything about the rumor I heard about Walker, or about my suspicions about his illegal dealing. It might have nothing to do with Kyle's disappearance, and I need the police to do their jobs and track down any other possible leads.

Then the detective asks me to wait in the room, and they leave to go interview Carla. As the door closes behind me, I rest my head in my hands and stare into space. The reality of the situation hits me.

Hard.

I start to sob, and I'm grateful the tears are flowing.

They're watching me, I'm sure.

And this will surely count in my favor.

I'M DRIVING HOME NOW. Carla's cleared, as well as Eddie's two employees, and it seems as if nothing further will come of it as far as they're concerned. All three of them have alibis that checked out for the time of my attack and Kyle's disappearance.

I'm relieved. I still have no idea what Carla meant when she mouthed to me that she had my back. I don't know if she was trying to keep something from Roger or warn me that the police were trying to get her to cooperate.

But we all drove separately, and she left before Roger came back into the interview room to update me. I can't ask her about it over the phone or via text. They're still monitoring my phone, in case a ransom demand comes in, which seems more and more unlikely as the hours pass.

I'm trying to make sense of it all. If someone wanted to kill Kyle, why would they take me, too? Were they hoping that if they got me, they could use me to coerce him into giving them money? Or were we simply in the wrong place at the wrong time as the detective seemed to suggest?

Again, I don't believe in coincidences. And now that I've had a cry about the possibility that Kyle might be gone, I need to look out for myself. I'm going to set up a meeting with Wes Walker and try to take his skin temperature on the stalled development project. If I can give him some assurance that he'll get his money back, I'll be much safer.

Because I've thought more about what Roger said. That I should consider the possibility that Kyle was going to bump me off and use the insurance on me to pay off his debts. It still could have been Kyle on that tape, and I'm not giving up trying to figure out who the woman was that Kyle was meeting. She could be his lover. Affairs happen all the time. Why would we be immune to one? Perhaps I never went far enough for Kyle, and he turned elsewhere.

And Roger got back to me with an answer to my question about life insurance. It's not easy to get paid out if there's no body—except in cases where there's enough evidence to conclude that someone is dead. Judging from the amount of blood they found at the hotel and in Kyle's car,

Roger thinks I might be able to get a provisional death certificate.

And a payout.

So, first thing tomorrow morning, I'm going to Wes Walker's office to get ahead of this. I need to protect myself, and if I can buy myself some time and let him know I've got a plan to get his money, I'll be safer, whether or not he had anything to do with Kyle's disappearance.

The crowd of reporters outside my home starts to part for me as I pull into the driveway towards my garage. Waiting for the garage door to rise, I glance in my rearview mirror. The driver in the car parked across the street catches my eye, just as she pulls away from the curb.

I gasp, and my stomach lurches. It's the brunette woman from Carla's photo. The woman my husband met at a coffee shop. The woman who went to a hotel with Kyle in the middle of the day. *What the hell is she doing camped outside my house?*

"Is Mr. Walker in?" I ask the receptionist. The building itself is massive, with the warehouse comprising most of the square footage. The office is functional, nothing fancy. But it's nicer than one would expect for a building supply headquarters. Modern, if a bit dated, with glass block, leather furnishings, and a stunning dark wood reception desk, which appears to be made of ebony.

"Who should I say is calling?"

"Morgan Murphy. I'm Kyle Murphy's wife," I say. "My husband is Mr. Walker's associate."

Her eyebrows rise. I imagine that she's putting two and two together—and that she watches the evening news.

"Is he expecting you?" she asks.

"No," I say.

"Please take a seat. I'll see what I can do."

She motions to a pair of black leather club chairs side by side in the lobby, with a teak end table between them. I follow her instructions.

It's late in the day. I didn't want to take off from work to meet him, so went to work early, left a little after five, and took a chance that he'd still be here. They told me to take all the time I need, but I know that's HR speak. The firm's about making money, and I don't want to be replaced. Plus, sticking to my routine grounds me.

This morning, Roger and I met for a bit about my suspicions. It seems that going after the illegal wood importing business is a major priority for the feds right now. There's a joint task force: TIMBER, an acronym for a bunch of federal agencies united to crack down on the practice. And it's way more complicated than I imagined. Even if you're trying to do the right thing, global supply chains are complex, and it's hard to know exactly where the wood originates, especially if you're dealing with foreign governments and businesses.

Roger pointed out that it also makes my situation more dangerous, because in some cases, illegal timber money is tied up in other sorts of more lethal enterprises, like the drug trade, which is run by cartels. So, it's quite possible that Walker is just the tip of the iceberg—and much less of a threat than what lurks underneath the surface.

I've called Carla several times, starting with last night when I saw the brunette woman outside my house. She's not returning my phone calls. Roger assured me that I had nothing to worry about as far as the police investigation and Carla. If they did try and flip her, he's sure she stayed quiet, or they would have gone after me much harder. But I don't like it. Something seems off, and I've never felt so alone.

After ten minutes or so, the receptionist calls out to me. "He'll see you now," she says. She directs me to his office.

He's a formidable man, mid-fifties, who looks like he

could have been a cowboy or a sheriff in the Wild West, with weathered skin that he wears well. He's old school California, and his family goes back a few generations. He's striking: tan, tall, and fit, from what I can tell, dressed in jeans and a navy pullover with a collared shirt underneath.

"Mrs. Murphy," he says, as he stands up to greet me. "Has there been any news about your husband?"

"None, I'm afraid."

He shakes his head. "Sorry to hear that. Please." He motions to the brown leather chair in front of his massive wooden desk, mahogany if I had to guess. "Take a seat."

We both sit.

"Thank you. I'm sorry to barge in on you like this. But I thought we should talk."

He sits back in his chair, brow furrowed. "About?"

I take a deep breath. "I know you're one of Kyle's investors. In his new project. And I wanted to assure you that no matter what, I'll make sure you recover your investment."

"Seems like a strange thing to have on your mind, with all you have going on," he says.

An uncomfortable silence settles over the office, and I fear that this might be a terrible idea. What if he senses that I'm suspicious about him?

"There's not much I can do about that. The police are handling the investigation. Meanwhile, life goes on." I shrug.

He nods, an agreeable nod that seems to suggest he's impressed with me. "That it does. But it seems a little premature to write off your husband."

My stomach sinks. "I'm not writing him off, Mr. Walker.

Just trying to be proactive. I thought a man like you would appreciate that."

He narrows his eyes on me. "A man like me? Meaning?"

I take a deep breath. "A businessman," I reply.

"Oh. Well, I'm not heartless, Mrs. Murphy. I know you have a lot on your plate. I can wait. But it's big of you to allay my concerns. And smart, too. I know you're a smart lady. I remember that about you."

"Please. Call me Morgan," I say, my brain taking a moment to catch up to what he just said. "You remember me? From my old firm?"

"You're not an easy woman to forget."

Brushing off the mild flirtation, I continue. "I'm smart enough to know that my husband probably told you that the zoning change was a sure thing. But it wasn't. And it didn't go through, and with him missing, the project can't move forward. Time is money. Your money. And I want you to know that I understand that. I'll make it a priority to make you whole. You don't need to worry about that."

He smiles now, a hearty smile that reaches the eyes. "I like you, Morgan Murphy. I like your style. And for the record, I wasn't worried about that. But what if I don't want to be made whole?" he says.

"Huh?"

"What if I want to try and salvage this project? With you as my partner?"

"I don't know much about this business, Mr. Walker."

"But I do."

"Let me think about it," I reply.

"Is there anything else?" he asks.

And now, my theory that he may have harmed Kyle

seems more unlikely. What would this guy have to gain from Kyle's death? He doesn't know about the life insurance, and he wants to move forward with the project.

But then, who could it be?

My mind flashes to the woman in front of my house yesterday. Could she have done something to Kyle? Perhaps it's not financial. Maybe he tried to break it off with her and she freaked out. Hired someone to try and get rid of me. Or both of us.

"No," I reply.

"You think about my offer and get back to me," he says.

I stand. "Thanks for your time, Mr. Walker. Have a nice day."

"Call me Wes," he says, eyeing me with a sly smile and a twinkle in his eye, although he's wearing a wedding band.

"Wes, it is." I offer him a polite half-smile and pull my cardigan tight around my body. I need to be careful. I don't want him getting the wrong idea. It's the last thing I need right now.

"You remind me a little of my daughter," he says. "She's a little younger than you, but she's got that same spunky attitude. Just like her mama. I mean that as a compliment. I like strong women."

"Thanks," I say. "I'll see myself out."

That makes me feel a little better. It could be that I'm oversensitive to the come-on vibe, after everything that's happened to me. I'm not writing him off as a possible perpetrator, but I need more information. Still, I'm feeling more hopeful after our visit, and I breathe a small sigh of relief as I head out the door, looking forward to an uneventful evening at home.

I'VE GOT no food in the house, so I need to stop at Safeway on the way home. As I pull out of the parking lot after my meeting, a car starts up and follows me. I find this odd because nobody came out ahead of me or behind me, so this person must have been sitting in their car, waiting. It's a dark blue Ford Focus, older but well kept. I think it's a man in the driver's seat, but it's hard to tell.

People do sit in their cars, I tell myself, trying not to give in to the paranoia. Perhaps he was returning a call or pulling up directions on his phone. I speed up a bit and the car hangs back. Then I take a right turn, and the car doesn't follow me.

After a few more rights and lefts, I make my way to Stevens Creek Boulevard and join the flow of traffic, getting over in the left lane so I can make the turn towards Safeway. As I stop at a traffic light, I glance in my rearview mirror, and I swear I spot the car again. But I can't be sure, because it's a few cars back. My stomach tightens as the left arrow turns green and I make the turn, my eyes darting back and forth between the rearview mirror and the car in front of me.

It dawns on me that any crazy person could be after me. I've made myself a public figure, and with my spicy marriage interview and my husband missing, I'm an easy mark. It was a rash move, and probably foolish. But what choice did I have? If one of the guys we hired went public with it first, I'd be in worse trouble.

I breathe through the wave of panic, telling myself that I'll be safe in a public place. It's broad daylight, and nobody will attack me now. After a few blocks, I pull into the Safeway parking lot. I find a spot near the front and pull into a space. With my hands shaking, I turn off the engine, grab my purse, and head in. There's no sign of the dark blue Focus, but it's a big lot. I make a mental note to get some pepper spray and have it with me at all times. Perhaps I should think about leaving town. Starting over.

After I collect the insurance money.

Once inside, I start to relax. I make my way around the store, throwing my usuals into the cart: wheat bread, broccoli, arugula, tomatoes, carrots. I spot a bag of red potatoes and go to grab them, thinking of how much Kyle likes those, roasted with garlic. My breath catches as reality hits me like a ton of bricks. The room spins, and I need to steady myself by leaning on the cart. A woman with a toddler in her cart backs away from me, but an older man with kind eyes puts a hand on my shoulder.

"Are you okay?" he asks.

"Yes," I say. "Thank you."

But I'm not.

I remember this happening when my dad died. I'd forget for a moment that he was gone, like at school one day when I got the highest grade on a math test and I thought *I can't wait to tell my dad.* Then the grief hit me all over again, and it seemed so cruel. Today is just like that, and it's starting to dawn on me that I have nobody. Carla's abandoned me, and I have no family to speak of. And if Kyle's really gone forever? Where do I go from here?

Taking a deep breath, I leave that for another time. I've got bigger problems. Steadying myself, I move past the potatoes towards the dairy aisle. I open the door to grab a bottle of milk, and I can feel someone behind me.

"Hello, Morgan," a voice says. "You look a little shaky. Are you okay?"

I turn and see Eddie Flores standing there with a smirk on his face. He's a smaller guy, about five foot nine, with deep-set eyes and a small scar under his left eye, dressed in jeans and a blue t-shirt.

My stomach sinks.

What the hell does he want?

But I don't want to antagonize him, so I try to play nice. He's never liked me. Thinks I'm a bad influence on his wife.

"I'm fine, Eddie. Thanks for asking."

His face hardens, his eyes turning beady and cold. Like a shark's eyes. "I know what you did, Morgan. And you crossed a line, involving Carla."

"Eddie, it was a harmless—"

"Shut the fuck up, Morgan," he barks in a low whisper, his teeth clenched. "I know what you were planning. I found those pictures on Carla's phone, and she told me everything."

"I don't know what you're talking about."

"Don't play games with me, Morgan. The guys aren't stupid. They're threatening to go to the police and tell them they think it wasn't a hoax if I don't pay up. Carla could be in real trouble, all because of you."

"What do you want, Eddie?" I'm starting to tremble, but I try not to let it show.

"Money, Morgan. I want money. To shut them up. And to shut us up. Because I know how these things work. And I'm sure if Carla goes to the police and tells them about the affair, they'll give her immunity to testify against you. And then you're screwed."

"I didn't do anything to Kyle," I say.

"I don't believe you. And it doesn't matter anyway. We all know how it looks. And my wife's not going down for this."

"How much money?"

"A million dollars," he says.

"I don't have that kind of—"

"Find it, Morgan. I know about the life insurance, and I want to be first in line, ahead of Walker or whoever else your husband owes. A million dollars. Got it?"

The cold milk sweats in my hot hand as my pulse races. I search my brain for a clever retort but come up empty. He's holding all the cards, and we both know it.

After a few moments, I nod. "Okay, Eddie. I'll get you your money. But I need some time."

"You've got two weeks."

He turns and walks away.

I close the refrigerator door and lean against it, still holding the bottle of milk in my hand.

I'm so screwed.

PART 2

EIGHTEEN
TARA

Carla Flores is a ghost. I've been trying for two days, and she hasn't returned my phone calls. But I did happen to track down someone from Morgan Murphy's past who seems willing and even eager to talk to me. It's dinnertime, and I'm pulling up to her home now. She lives in a fifty-plus retirement complex in Los Gatos, a small town about thirty minutes south of Cupertino.

She buzzes me in. It's a low rise. Three stories. There's an elevator but it looks slow. I take the stairs, locate apartment 3F, and knock on the door.

A woman opens the door. Her hair is long and blonde, damaged from too much bleach, but she looks younger than I pictured her. She must be close to sixty, but she gives off a younger woman vibe. Maybe it's the outfit. Jeans and a long-sleeved red turtleneck sweater. I see the resemblance immediately.

"I'm Tara Harker," I say. "We spoke on the phone."

"Linda Anderson," she says. "Come in."

She offers me coffee, and I accept.

Black, I tell her.

It gives me some time to look around. I take a seat on the small beige leather loveseat. Her apartment is small but tidy, with dated furnishings in good repair. It lacks character, though. No photos, which is odd. What looks to be a signed print of a tropical landscape oil painting that appears to be somewhere in the Caribbean. No nicknacks. Nothing to indicate who this woman is or what makes her tick. That, in and of itself, tells me something.

After five minutes or so, she sets the coffee down in front of me and takes a seat on the matching recliner. "So, I assume you're here to talk about my daughter," she says.

Cutting to the chase must run in the family.

"Yes, Mrs. Anderson," I say.

"Call me Linda."

I offer her a warm smile. "As you know, Linda, your daughter's husband is missing. Have you been in touch with her?"

She shakes her head. "I haven't seen Morgan in nearly two decades." She lowers her eyes, seemingly embarrassed by that admission. Then she looks back up at me. "How... how is she? How's she handling it all?"

"She seems to be holding up okay, given the circumstances," I reply.

There's an awkward silence, and I get the feeling that I'm here more to give information than to get it. She seems desperate for news of her daughter, and I gather that the estrangement is more on Morgan's side. I need to get her talking. Get her to loosen up.

"That's a lovely painting," I say, gesturing towards the print. "Where is that?"

She forces a smile, as if the memory is bittersweet. "St. Croix."

"Have you been there?" I ask.

Her face softens. "Twice. We went on our honeymoon. Morgan's dad and I. And then again when Morgan was around six. Before her father passed away."

"He passed when she was a child?"

She nods. "Morgan was only seven."

"Tough," I say.

"Yes. She took it hard. They were very close."

"I'm sorry for your loss," I say. She catches my eye, and we both understand that I'm talking about her daughter as well as her husband.

"Thank you," she says.

Something must have triggered the estrangement from Morgan, so I venture a guess. "Did you remarry?" I ask.

She tells me that she did, a few years after her husband's death. And she reveals that there was some friction between Morgan and her stepdad, which escalated when Morgan entered her teen years.

"You know how teenagers can be," she says. "Hormones and all that."

"I do," I reply.

But something else happens when girls hit their teen years. *Puberty.*

Putting this information together with Morgan's self-defense skills and the fact that she doesn't speak to her mother, I wonder if the stepdad did something to Morgan.

Something creepy that would make her vow to never be defenseless again. Perhaps she blames her mother for not protecting her. It wouldn't be the first time.

I came here to get dirt on Morgan, but suddenly I'm feeling protective of her. Perhaps I'm personalizing it, and I remind myself not to let my past experiences taint my powers of analysis. But I'm picking up a vibe. Linda Anderson feels guilty about something, I'm sure of that. And I want to know what it is.

Morgan's mother continues. "Eventually, we divorced. Morgan put a strain on our marriage, but that wasn't the only reason. I've never loved anyone the way I loved Morgan's father. And it was hard for Jim, my second husband, because he sensed it. Even though I tried my best to bury those feelings. But you didn't come to hear my sob story. What did you want to talk to me about?"

"I'm looking for background on Morgan. To try and understand her better. And to flesh out the story of Kyle Murphy's disappearance."

She rests her head in her hands for a minute before she speaks again. Then she sighs. "I tried my best with her, Ms. Harker, but obviously I should have done more. And this is all my fault. I should have gotten her help, but I was such a mess. The grief. It consumed me, and I had nothing left for my daughter." Her chin trembles, as if she's about to break down, but she sucks it back in.

I put my hand on her arm. "Call me Tara," I say. "What's all your fault, Linda? What could you have done more about?"

She looks off to the side, twirling a few strands of straw-colored hair between her fingers, then turns back to me.

"Her anger," Linda says. "At me. For good reason. And at her dad, for dying. She never accepted her stepfather."

"That sounds pretty normal."

She takes a deep breath, as if she's having second thoughts about letting me in. But then she continues. "No. There's something I found out later. Years after it happened. If I'd known at the time, I would have put Morgan in therapy. But Jim didn't tell me until after she'd moved out. I kept trying to reach out to Morgan, and he was tired of seeing me get slapped in the face. He wanted me to cut my losses. So, then he finally told me."

"Told you what?"

Her wide eyes search mine for some kind of confirmation that she should continue. "I want this to be off the record. Can you assure me of that?"

Damn. It was going so well.

"Um, sure, Linda. Off the record."

"That means you won't put it in your news report, right?"

"That's right," I assure her.

She swallows. "Morgan stabbed her stepdad in the thumb. When she was fourteen. At the time, he told me it was an accident. That he'd cut himself making dinner. But I suppose, looking back, I should have known. It didn't look like the kind of injury you could give yourself. But people see what they want to see, I guess."

That's for sure.

Because I doubt that a fourteen-year-old girl would stab her stepdad in the hand for no reason at all. Yet again, you never know. Either there's a story there and the stepdad was some kind of pervert, or Morgan Murphy is a psychopath. Any way you slice it, it's a juicy story.

"She has anger issues, my daughter. She's the jealous type. I think she was jealous of Jim. He took me away from her. And now her husband is missing. I told myself I wouldn't go to the police, but if they came, I'd tell them what I know. But you came first. And here we are. Are you going to tell them?"

"It's not really my place," I say. "It's hearsay, and it wouldn't be the kind of evidence they could use."

"So, what are you going to do with the information?" she asks.

That's a fair question.

I know what I'm going to do with it, but I'm not telling Linda Anderson. "I'll keep it to myself for now," I lie.

And then she clams up. Mutters something about going to meet a friend and starts to usher me out of the house, as if she's having second thoughts about her admission.

Guilt can be like that. You're desperate to get something off your chest, even if you know it's a bad move. Even if you sense it will make things worse. Like telling your spouse you cheated, because it's eating you alive to keep it inside. It gives you relief for a moment, and then the implications kick in and you wish you could take it all back.

Any chance of reconciliation with her daughter probably flew out the window if I don't keep this to myself, and she knows it. Does she really believe her daughter is dangerous? Or is she in denial, and this is her way of rationalizing the fact that she failed to protect her own flesh and blood?

NINETEEN
MORGAN

Pulling the covers over my head, I try to ignore the beam of light peering through my window, indicating that it's time to start my day. It's well past the time I should be up and out the door, but I'm curled up in a ball in the middle of our bed, hiding from the world. I haven't washed the sheets since the incident because they smell of Kyle. But his scent is starting to fade, like the hope that I might see him alive again.

I tell myself to be strong. But for what? I've made Kyle my world, and now that he's missing, I'm all alone. Like I was right after my father died.

My mother cleaned herself up a few months after his death, but the first few months were agonizing. She couldn't get out of bed. The house was a disaster. Dishes piled up in the sink, if we used them at all. Mostly, I was left to fend for myself, living on pop tarts and hot pockets while she wallowed in grief and guilt. I'm surprised I didn't get scurvy.

She wasn't mean to me or anything. More like distant, as if her maternal instincts had been snuffed out by her miscarriage and my father's death. She didn't seem like a mom. Moms were strong and brave and there for you. I remember watching sitcoms and wishing my mom was like the ones I saw on TV. I wanted her to tell me to eat my vegetables and go to bed on time and give me time-outs when I was sassy. But all she did was stumble around from room to room, sometimes not showering for days, in a medication- and alcohol-induced stupor.

But she loved me, in her own weird way. Sometimes she'd sneak into my room, late at night, and kiss the top of my head. I could smell the scotch on her breath, and I grew to like it. How sad is that? Now the smell of it makes me sick. I couldn't invite friends over. It was all too embarrassing for me.

But a few months after the funeral, she started to change. She quit drinking. Went back to work. And although she was no June Cleaver, things were better for a few years. She worked a lot, but that was fine with me. Our home was basic but clean. She smelled of vanilla body lotion instead of scotch. Then one day she said she had a surprise for me.

"A surprise?" I asked. I'd been bugging her to go to Disneyland. I was nine years old at the time. It was my ultimate dream vacation. All the kids I knew had been there except me, and I thought I might finally get my turn.

"Yes. And I know this might be hard for you. But it's a good thing. Trust me."

Hard for me?

That didn't sound good.

My heart started to race. "Am I in trouble?"

I'd read a story about a boy who got sent away to boarding school because his family didn't want him around.

But I had a feeling that cost a lot of money, and we didn't seem to have much of it. Whatever this was, it didn't seem like I was going to Disneyland.

She took a deep breath, placed her hands on my shoulders, and looked me in the eye. "I've met someone," she said. "His name is Jim."

"Oh," I said.

My stomach sank.

She'd been dressing better lately. Wearing more make-up. Smiling. I thought it was because of me. I was doing well in school, although she didn't seem to notice. But it wasn't me. It was some guy named Jim who was going to replace my dad.

Then a thought occurred to me. Maybe he had kids. That wouldn't be so bad. I'd seen reruns of *The Brady Bunch*. Maybe it would be like that show, and I'd have silly brother-sister fights and then we'd make up and laugh about how silly it was and I wouldn't be so lonely anymore.

"Are you okay, Morgan?" she asked.

I realized we'd been standing in silence a long time. "Does he have any kids?" I asked.

"No. No kids. But he's really excited to meet you. He's coming for dinner tonight."

Tonight?

I took a deep breath and pushed down the wave of grief that was welling up about the loss of my dad. I wondered what she would do with the pictures of him around our house. Would she put them away? Would she let me keep the ones I had near my bed? But then another thought popped into my head, and I decided to try and make the best of it. Because at heart, I'm an optimist.

"Do you think he wants to go to Disneyland?" I asked.

A dazzling smile as bright as the sun burst onto my mom's face. I hadn't seen her smile like that since forever.

I took that as a yes.

"Oh, Morgan. Yes. Whatever you want. I'm sure he'd love that."

She reached for me and hugged me tight and kissed the top of my head. I was suddenly very excited to meet this Jim guy and start a new life as a family, just like the ones I saw on TV. And finally get my trip to Disneyland. Which they made good on, by the way, so at least there's that.

But as I reflect on my mother moping around in her bedclothes, wallowing in self-pity, I'm snapped out of my lethargy. I've spent my whole life trying not to be her. I called in sick last night after running into Eddie, feeling totally overwhelmed, and my stomach sinks at the thought that I'm now following in her footsteps. I regret it now, calling in sick, but I've got the day off, and I'm going to make the most of it.

I hop out of bed, throw off the comforter, rip our pale blue satin sheets off our mattress, pull the pillows out of their cases, and head for the laundry room. On my way, I see I've got a bunch of texts and one voicemail—from Tara Harker. I play it immediately, almost tripping over a pair of shoes I left strewn on the floor, the laundry piled up in my arms.

She wants to meet with me today.

What could she possibly want from me now?

I HAVE to face the fact that Kyle is gone, and it's not my job to try and find him. It's my job to protect myself. I've scrubbed the house clean, fed myself a breakfast of oatmeal, fruit, and nuts, and I'm ready to move forward, fueled by two cups of coffee. I've got two weeks to get Eddie the money. Taking out a mortgage or a loan might trigger the police to look into me, and I don't need that. My only option is to figure out a way to collect the life insurance money, so I'll start there.

I also need to get back to Wes Walker on his proposal. If I can string him along, I won't have to worry about paying him off. But I'd rather make a clean break. I'll stall as long as I can, and if I can get the life insurance money, I'll pay him off and let him take it from there as far as the project is concerned.

Setting up a meeting with Roger is my next step. He can help me figure out the life insurance. Grabbing my phone to call him, I notice another message from Tara Harker, and I let out a sigh. Perhaps I should call her. She might know something about the case that I don't know. Reporters have their ways of getting information.

I'm still very curious about the mystery brunette. Why was she in front of my house? What was she doing with my husband? And I feel guilty for keeping that from the police. What if she had something to do with his disappearance? But I can't let on about her, because then they'll know I had my suspicions about Kyle—and a motive to murder him. I'd rather blow my brains out than spend a day in prison.

But maybe there's something Tara Harker knows that can give me a clue as to who she is and what was going on. If I could get her to uncover the cheating on her own, or somehow figure out why they were meeting, and if she told the police, then it wouldn't land back on me. I'd have to put on a great act when she told me. Crumble visibly before her eyes at the thought of Kyle's betrayal. But I could pull it off. As I said, I'm a great actress.

And I *am* crushed, after all. That part isn't an act. About his disappearance. And about the fact that I might never know whether Kyle was unfaithful to me or not.

"Hi, Morgan," she says, picking up on the second ring. "Thanks for getting back to me."

"Hi, Tara. What can I do for you?"

"I was hoping I could stop by and ask you some questions."

"Have there been any developments on the case?"

"I'd rather talk about it in person," she replies.

"Off camera?" I ask.

"Yes. Just the two of us. Maybe after work?"

"I'm off today, so you can come by any time."

"I, um, I'm actually working, but I can come around six. Would that work?"

She's working?

Isn't she a reporter?

What does she mean by that?

"Sure, six works."

We hang up, and I think about what this signifies. Kyle's disappearance might not be her assignment. I have no idea how that works at a news station. But if she's so obsessed with me and this case that she's coming here on her own time, that could be great for me.

Or it could be terrible.

Depending on what she uncovers.

But I push that thought aside to call Roger and find out what my next steps should be on the life insurance. I need a million dollars and I've only got two weeks.

The clock is ticking.

One week and six days.

"Is Detective Rodman in?" I ask.

"And you are?" the desk officer asks.

"Morgan Murphy. I'm here about my husband's case. Kyle Murphy's his name. Missing persons case."

"Wait over there," he says, pointing to the seating area. Then he picks up the phone and calls someone, but it doesn't seem like anyone answered.

It appears as if everyone's forgotten about my case. The police are eerily quiet. The media is no longer camped outside my home. I should be grateful for Tara Harker. At least she hasn't given up on finding out what happened to Kyle.

Roger and I talked about the life insurance, and he said it all depends on what they found. I checked our policy, and there's a provision in it for a payout in the event of someone going missing with no body, if there's compelling evidence that they're dead, such as someone falling off a boat and never being seen again. But I can't open with: *Hey, did you find enough blood to trigger the life insurance policy I have on my husband?*

He also counseled me that I need to keep pressure on the police department. Pump them for information. It's what a family member is expected to do in this kind of situation, he says. If I back off and let them do their jobs, it will look bad, like I don't care. And I can't let on that I'm after bad news so that I can collect the life insurance policy. I have to appear to be a concerned family member. Which I am.

A concerned family member with a ticking time bomb strapped to my body.

It's a quiet day, which makes me more antsy. The officer keeps glancing over at me like he's afraid I'll leave, but nobody comes. I've been neglecting my social media accounts, so I pass the time checking up on them. I'm pleased to see that my advice helped someone. The man who contacted me about his new baby dilemma sent me a message.

> My husband accepted my date night offer. He was also wanting some alone time, but he wasn't sure how I felt. Thanks for giving me permission to put my marriage front and center. Hope things get better for you soon. I can't imagine how you're even holding up at all, never mind taking time to help us. Thanks again.

This makes me feel positive about myself for the first time in over a week, and I start to write back. I'm interrupted before I can fire off my reply.

"Mrs. Murphy?" Detective Rodman calls out. "You can come with me."

I tuck my phone in my purse and head towards him. We walk in silence, and the various ways I can play this run through my head.

Angry.

Frightened.

Vulnerable.

My gut tells me that this guy is pretty no-nonsense, so I could always be direct.

"What can I do for you?" he asks, as we get seated in a conference room. It's small and functional, but not intimidating. Not like the other room I was in that's used to grill suspects. I take it as a good sign that he brought me here. Hopefully, I'm no longer under suspicion.

"Has there been any new information in my husband's case?" I say.

"Nothing but what I've shared with you," he replies.

"Is that common? That there would be no news?"

"These things take time, Mrs. Murphy."

I roll my eyes, letting my natural personality take over. "My life is a mess, Detective Rodman. Someone tried to kill me. I'm terrified all the time. What are you doing to protect me?"

He sighs. "I've instructed our officers to do regular patrols of your neighborhood and your home. We're on the lookout for the man who attacked you. But I'm afraid we don't have a budget to station someone at your home all the time. Have you thought about private security?"

I let out a huff, expressing my exasperation. "We're not wealthy, Detective. We're not Silicon Valley billionaires. My husband works on commission, and he owes a lot of money on his project, which can't move forward. I don't know how long I can last on a paralegal's salary. This is an expensive area. We have life insurance. We don't have 'disappearing spouse' insurance. Or 'someone tried to kill me and I need security at my home' insurance."

He opens his mouth as if he's about to speak, but nothing comes out. He seems to be at a momentary loss for words. There's a sympathetic look on his face, though. I think. Or maybe that's just how he looks. He's very attractive, in a pleasant sort of way, and I have to be careful not to let that lull me into a false sense of security. This could be his good-cop strategy.

My hand goes to my forehead. "I'm sorry, I just feel so powerless. And I hate it. I'm angry at Kyle for leaving me with this mess. I know that's crazy, because it's not his fault. But that's how I feel."

That's the truth, and from the look on his face, my plight seems to resonate with him.

"I'm sorry, Mrs. Murphy. It's a common reaction. Anger. Missing persons cases are tough. Because with a death, you can grieve and move on. But in this instance, you reexperience it over and over. Victim's services should be in touch with you soon. They have support groups they can recommend, if that sort of thing interests you."

I sigh. "Not yet. That feels like I'm giving up. Are you giving up? On Kyle?"

Rodman looks away and then back at me. "We're not giving up on finding out who did this to your husband."

"That isn't what I asked you. What are the chances he's still alive?"

There's a prolonged silence. He looks up at the ceiling and blows out a breath. "It doesn't look encouraging, with the amount of blood we found. And the fact that he hasn't surfaced yet. And that there's been no ransom demand. But you never know, so don't give up hope."

Wringing my hands, I struggle to get my brain around this. He's basically telling me that Kyle's dead. "What if I never know what happened? I don't think I can handle it. What about your theory? That Kyle was a victim of that ring of carjackers? Have you made any headway?"

"They've been quiet, so that is an indication to me that I might be right. As I said, they don't normally kill people, so if it went south, they could have moved on. Geographically. Or strategically, with some other kind of plan."

"What should I do?" I ask.

"I can't really answer that," he says. "I don't know you that well, or your situation. Maybe you could move in with a friend? Or get a dog?"

I nod my head in agreement.

A dog isn't a bad idea.

And maybe a gun.

"Let me rephrase my question," I say. "What would you do if you were me?"

"Have you checked your life insurance policy? Sometimes they'll pay out in the event of a missing person case, if there's enough evidence that the person is dead."

I struggle to hide the feeling of exuberance bubbling up inside of me. I keep a somber look on my face, but it's not easy. My smile muscles are about to burst at the seams. I can't believe he brought it up.

"Yes. We have a clause like that," I say. "But I need something called a provisional death certificate. Or I have to wait five years. I'll be bankrupt by then."

"That might be possible to get, given the circumstances. But if your husband is found alive, you'd have to pay the money back."

"I'd gladly give everything I have and more to have my husband home with me again. But in the meantime, I need to put food on the table. And keep myself safe."

We run through the procedure involved in obtaining a provisional death certificate, and I can't believe my luck. I don't ask how long it will take, and I'm sure it will be longer than two weeks. But if I can assure Eddie that the money's coming, I might be able to buy myself some time. Only an idiot would pull the trigger by going to the police and turning me in, missing out on a million-dollar payout.

And Eddie's not an idiot.

TARA HARKER IS due here in half an hour, and I need to do something to distract myself. I never did get back to the married guy with the baby. Reading his message again, I'm struck by the fact that I've positively impacted someone's life, and it didn't take much effort. I've never given much thought to the idea of being a YouTube star or a social media influencer or an advice columnist. But perhaps I should think about it.

> I'm so glad it helped. Keep the fires burning. There's nothing better for your child than a healthy relationship.

There's a message from the woman who was worried that her husband might be cheating, telling me that it's going well so far. I respond with a smiley face emoji. There are a few more DMs from strangers, and part of me wants to ignore them and quit while I'm ahead. I'm bound to come across a lunatic sooner or later. But of course, curiosity gets the best of me, so I start reading them.

Hi there.

Probably some kind of AI bot, looking to scam me. I delete it and move on.

If you're bored or lonely, hit me up.

Ewe. Gross. *Delete.*

I move on to the next one, mentally reversing course, thinking that this social media influencer idea is possibly the worst one I've ever had. You have to take the good with the bad, and I'm sure there's a lot of bad out there. One more, and I'll call it quits. Tara should be here soon, anyway.

You may have fooled the police, but you didn't fool me. And you're going to get yours.

I slam the computer down. It's probably Eddie, trying to rattle me. *Asshole.* It worked, though. I'm officially rattled, but I don't want to lose my cool in front of Tara Harker. I stand up and take some deep breaths, trying to slow my racing heart. I need to find a way to get a message to Eddie that I'm going to get his money to him.

The doorbell rings, so I leave it for the time being and greet my new best friend at the door. I don't have many female friends, aside from Carla. And seeing as how her husband is trying to blackmail me, I'm guessing that a girl's lunch is now off the table.

Tara and I amuse each other, but we've got more of a frenemy vibe going. We're too alike to really be friends, but we get one another. I sense we're cut from the same cloth. She's out for herself, like everyone. But she's upfront about it, which I respect. I ask her in and we get settled. She declines refreshments, and it seems like she's in a bit of a rush. Maybe she needs to be somewhere, or she's just anxious to talk to me.

"Thanks for agreeing to talk to me, Morgan," she says.

I don't like the sound of that. Why is she kissing up to me? Does she know something I don't know?

"Um, sure, Tara. What can I do for you?"

She takes a deep breath, looks away, and then looks back at me. "I've been doing some background on you. For a more in-depth piece we want to do on Kyle's case."

On me?

Why me?

"And when is this...piece coming out?" I ask.

"We're not sure yet. It's in the development stage."

I don't believe her. I think she's fishing, trying to dig something up so she can get the station to let her work on it. Something sensational that would get ratings, like my last interview. Why else would she be coming after hours?

But I play along. "I see."

There's a prolonged silence. I keep my eyes trained on her, waiting for her to move on.

She swallows. "I interviewed someone during the course of my investigation. And this person told me something. Off the record, which means I've agreed not to go public with it."

My stomach sinks.

Did Eddie or one of the guys go to her behind my back? But why would they do that when the money is coming? Was it the brunette, trying to get me in trouble? But I remain calm, I think. I don't know how I'm coming off to her. I remind myself about my mean resting face and force the corners of my mouth into a pleasant smile, and I'm sure I now look like one of the pod people in *Invasion of the Body Snatchers.*

"What is it? Is it something about Kyle's disappearance?" I ask.

"It's about you," she says. "Something from your past."

"From *my* past?" My mind races, thinking about what she could possibly be talking about. My creepy boss from years ago? Has he gone on the offensive, with all the media attention? Trying to kick me when I'm down? But I've got dirt on him. Why would he take that kind of risk?

"I went to see your mother," she says.

"What?" I'm seething.

Instantly.

And I can feel my blood pressure rise. It's showing, too.

Her eyes widen. "Calm down, Morgan," she says.

I spring up, cradling my head in my hands. "Why in the hell would you go see her? You had no right!"

I knew this woman was trouble.

"Morgan. Please sit. She told me something. And I wanted to get your side of the story."

"I want you to leave, Tara. *Now.* I thought you wanted to

help me, but you've been sneaking around behind my back. Trying to get dirt on me."

"Let me explain," she says.

I want to throw her out on her ass, but then I realize it's not in my best interest. I need to know what mommy dearest told her.

"You have two minutes," I say, taking a seat on the edge of my chair, making it clear that I mean what I said.

"She told me about your childhood. Losing your father when you were so young. I'm so sorry. And that you didn't have a great relationship with your stepfather."

"So? What does this have to do with Kyle? Or his disappearance."

"Well, she mentioned that there was an incident. When you were fourteen."

My stomach sinks.

Because I know exactly where this is going.

"She told me you stabbed him in the thumb with a kitchen knife. But she didn't find out until years later."

That bastard! He must have told her. I wondered why her calls dropped off so suddenly. I thought she just gave up on me. I'm sure he didn't tell her *why* I stabbed him.

Of course not.

"She's a drunk and he's a psycho. It's total bullshit. That never happened. You can't prove anything anyway. He's dead. Now leave, Tara. And don't come back."

"Morgan, I—"

"Leave!"

"Now!"

I pull her up from the sofa by the wrist, then push her towards the front door. Well, not so much push her. More like guide her. The last thing I need is a lawsuit on my hands. Can you imagine? As I'm closing the door behind her, she's still talking.

"I want to help, Morgan."

"Sure, Tara. Whatever you say." I try to close the door, but she sticks her foot in the threshold and peeks at me through the crack.

"Maybe he deserved it, Morgan. If he did, I understand."

"Nothing happened, Tara. You need to get a life and stop obsessing about mine. Now go."

But we hold each other's gaze for a few long moments, and I can see the concern in her eyes. She's genuinely worried about me. Briefly, I think about telling her everything. It would be better for me, strategically. If I told her the reason I stabbed him, she would understand. But then I'd have to admit to doing it. And that wouldn't be prudent. Right now, there's no proof.

I can't deal with this right now.

"Please go, Tara."

"Okay. But be careful, Morgan," she says. "I'm telling you this because your mother is thinking about going to the police about it. I wanted to give you a chance to get ahead of it."

She removes her foot and goes on her way. I close the door, turn around, and lean on it. Maybe Tara Harker's not so bad after all. My mother is a different story.

And then the tears start to flow.

A long time ago, a terrible thing happened. I was in eleventh grade. My best friend was a girl named Clarissa Moreland. She was a new friend, relatively speaking. We'd come from different middle schools that fed into the same high school. We'd met in journalism club the year before and worked together on the school newspaper.

I wasn't as confident then as I am now. I was on the shy side. She was flashy and bright and full of life, the kind of girl who lit up the room, and I wanted to be like her. She wore clothes with patterns and bright colors and laughed with abandon. A senior guy I had my eye on for over a year asked her out, our junior year. She said no, which shocked me, as well as the rest of the school. He wasn't the kind of guy you turned down.

I asked her why and she shrugged. "I'm in the market for someone more sophisticated." Then she gave her head a little shake and her light blonde bob followed, a second or two behind. When we met, she had long hair the color of spun gold, but she'd recently cut it shorter and lightened it a little. It did make her look older. Perhaps that was the objective?

I had no idea what she meant by that, but suddenly Danny Bristol didn't seem too appealing to me, either. If he wasn't good enough for Clarissa, I didn't want her leftovers.

Her family had money, unlike mine. But they were eccentric. I wouldn't have used that word at the time, but looking back, that's what they were. Eccentric rich people who had very strange opinions about child-rearing. I envied her at the time. Her mother told me she believed in permissive parenting and didn't give her daughter many, if any, rules or restrictions.

She was an only child, and her father traveled a lot, ostensibly for work. Her mother left her alone, sometimes for weeks on end. Yoga retreats. Tony Robbins workshops. European vacations. And Clarissa seemed fine fending for herself. She didn't have crazy parties or anything. Not like some of the other kids, and for a time I thought that her mother was on to something. She seemed pretty responsible to me. Chalk one up to permissive parenting.

One day, when her mother was out of town, I popped over to her house because she wasn't answering my phone calls or texts. It was about nine in the morning on a Saturday, and by this time, we were co-editors of the school paper. We were on a deadline, and neither of us wanted to disappoint our adviser, Mr. Suderman. He was well-liked and on the younger side. Friendly and approachable, but not in a creepy way. Attractive, with a square jaw, a nice smile, and light brown hair with a windswept look like he'd just come off the beach. He was the first adult to tell me I had potential as a journalist, and I wanted to please him. Plus, I planned to ask him to write my college recommendation, so I didn't want to disappoint him.

I rang the doorbell. Clarissa answered the door in a peach silk robe that sat just above the knee. This only served to make me more insecure. I slept in sweats and a t-shirt, and I wondered if I should shop for a new wardrobe before I went away to college. I didn't want to embarrass myself by looking like a middle school kid.

"What are you doing here?" she said.

"You weren't answering my calls. We have a deadline."

She rolled her eyes. "You need to get a life, Tara. I'm busy today. We can work on it tomorrow."

And she shut the door in my face.

I worried that I'd blown it with her. I wanted her to like me. I had other friends, but none of them dazzled me the way she did. There was something about her that fascinated me, and I sensed that something more was going on behind the scenes that morning. That was when I knew I had what it took to be an investigative reporter. I started looking at her as a story I needed to break.

Instead of going home, I sat in my car for a bit, across the street and down one house from hers, taking notes. I had a feeling that someone was in there with her, although there was no car in the driveway. My first thought was that it was Danny Bristol, the jock who she'd turned down. Maybe it was a secret rendezvous that they wanted to keep from the school. That seemed like something Clarissa would do. But, after a half hour or so, another car pulled into her driveway. A blue Honda Civic that looked vaguely familiar.

Mr. Suderman, our journalism adviser, got out of the car carrying two Starbucks coffees in his hands and a paper Starbucks bag on his wrist. Some coffee spilled on his hand as he closed the door with his hip. He wiped his hand on his pants and continued. He had bedhead hair and wore jeans and a t-shirt, which made him look younger than he did at school.

Clarissa opened the door and pulled him in for a kiss, and I felt like I was going to be sick. This was wrong. So wrong. And I had no idea what to do next. He'd get fired if I told the school, and she would never talk to me again.

And as much as I didn't want to make this about me, I have to admit that I thought about my college recommendation, too. I really needed Mr. Suderman to go to bat for me. If I told my mother, I'd be banned from journalism club and from seeing Clarissa, and I had a feeling she might need me at some point. I didn't see this having a fairy-tale ending.

I decided I'd wait for Clarissa's mother to get back to town and I'd tell her what was going on. Then she could put an end to it, and with that, her permissive parenting. It wouldn't come back to haunt me if Mr. Suderman was fired. After that day, I started to see my mother in a different light. As someone who wanted to protect me, even if it felt like overkill at the time.

So, I waited a week and didn't say anything to Clarissa. I tried to hide my disgust for Mr. Suderman. At least he wasn't married, but he had a girlfriend. He talked about her sometimes, because she was a photojournalist. He said it was a tough career path that required constant travel, and she was gone a lot, a comment I now saw as a pathetic excuse to seduce his young student.

I wasn't sure how Clarissa's mother would take this. She might perceive it as a criticism of her parenting, and I didn't want that.

"I have something to tell you, Mrs. Moreland," I said. We were in her living room, and she was wearing a flowing retro dress with a loud, swirly pattern that belonged in the seventies.

"Tara. Why so formal? I told you to call me Winnie. Now what's this about?"

I rolled my eyes. "*Winnie.* I have something to tell you. It's about Clarissa. And I'm warning you, it might be hard to hear."

Her face went pale and she clutched at her chest. "What is it? Is she sick? Is she on drugs or something?"

"No. Nothing like that." I swallowed. "But she's been seeing someone, and I thought you should know who it is."

Her brow furrowed. "You mean Gabe?" she asked.

My eyes nearly popped out of my head.

That was Mr. Suderman's first name.

She knew?

I stumbled through the rest of the conversation. She informed me that not only did she know about it, she approved of it. Clarissa was eighteen. She'd repeated a grade. And as far as Winnie was concerned, she could do as she pleased. Winnie was excited that her daughter was "finding herself" sexually. I felt like I was going to be sick and practically ran screaming from the house.

I had no idea what to do next. I mean, if her mother knew, it wasn't really my place to intervene, was it? But I started backing off from the friendship. The whole situation gave me the creeps. And I never did get that college recommendation.

Because I was right. It didn't end well. Mr. Suderman finally came to his senses and dumped Clarissa when he found out she was pregnant, second semester of our junior year. He offered to pay to "take care of it," but that wasn't what she wanted. Our friendship had cooled off, but I knew something was terribly wrong. She was absent from school for a week, near the end of the school year, and she dropped out of journalism club. I learned all of this in the girl's bathroom where I found her, crying her eyes out in a stall the day she came back.

Turns out, she wasn't sophisticated at all. She was a teenage girl, just like the rest of us, adopting the veneer of sophistication. She felt guilt. Remorse. Humiliation. Heartache. I tried to tell her it wasn't her fault, but she wouldn't have it. It all came out, and Mr. Suderman was escorted off campus the last week of school. That could have been the end of it.

But it wasn't.

The beginning of senior year, Clarissa got drunk and drove her car into a tree. I'd tried to befriend her again, but she wouldn't engage with me. She'd never been a big drinker, but the trauma must have pushed her over the edge. I could have done more. I should have reported it to the school. And I'll never forgive myself. I've been plagued with guilt ever since.

Morgan Murphy reminds me a little of Clarissa. They have a similar look. If Clarissa had grown up, she might look a bit like Morgan. And they've both closed a door in my face and told me to get a life. But it's not just that. They both seem tough on the outside, but I sense that Morgan, like Clarissa, is more fragile than she appears. Something about their mothers seems familiar too, although Linda Anderson doesn't have money or the free spirit vibe that Winnie had.

It's the willingness to turn a blind eye. To not protect your child and to see what you want to see. That's the common denominator.

That incident shaped me in other ways, too, and I'm sure that my insistence on supporting myself and my reluctance to fully commit to a relationship has its roots in that tragedy, seeing what losing yourself in a man could do to a person. It certainly wasn't my upbringing. My parents are a happy, normal couple, and Dad is my rock, although he's always encouraged me to rely on myself and be independent. Mom is another story, and I know she's disappointed that she has yet to shop for a mother of the bride dress.

I need to watch myself and try to remain objective, though. I don't want to be blinded to Morgan's dark side because I have some baggage from my high school days. But I have a hunch about Morgan's stepdad, and I need to find out more. I feel about Morgan the same way I felt about Clarissa. A sensation that trouble is around the corner. A morbid fascination, like watching a freight train that's about to crash into a brick wall. You know you should look away, but you can't.

That's how I felt, sitting in front of Clarissa's house that morning.

That's how I feel about Morgan now.

This isn't my assignment.

I have a job.

I need to get a life.

I need to look away.

But I can't.

TWENTY-TWO
MORGAN

I filed for the provisional death certificate the day after I went to the police station. I didn't ask how long it would take. I thought that might look suspicious. But I'm on pins and needles. It's been nearly a week and I haven't heard anything. And now that my past seems to be catching up with me, I'm thinking about starting a new life once I pay off Eddie and Wes Walker. Getting a new identity. Leaving town. Before anything more surfaces that could incriminate me. This reminds me that I haven't gotten back to Wes Walker about his partnership idea. I need to do that soon.

I'm at work, which is actually a godsend. I like to keep busy, and I'm good at what I do. Roger pops into my office. We've never talked about me or my case at work, so I suspect that he's got something new for me to work on. But then he closes the door, which he never does. He's got a serious look on his face. It's not easy for a giant baby to look serious, but he's pulling it off.

"Something's not sitting well with me, Morgan," he says, as he takes a seat in front of my desk.

"What do you mean?"

"I don't know. It seems too easy. Rodman telling you to file for a provisional death certificate so you could get the life insurance. I mean, who does that?"

I let out a sigh. That thought occurred to me, but I'm so desperate to pay off Eddie, I didn't let it settle for very long. "What are you getting at?"

"They could be using you to get to Kyle. Maybe they think you know where he is. And that this is some elaborate scheme you two cooked up to get the insurance money."

"Well, it isn't. I have no idea who took him or where he is. And someone tried to kidnap me. And Kyle's blood was all over the car. And how could we get the insurance money if they took both of us? There would be nobody to collect on the policies."

"True," he says. "But something doesn't smell right. Keep your guard up. Don't do anything rash with the money. Keep it in your bank account and use it for expenses, a little at a time. But don't be moving it anywhere, like a Swiss bank account."

Or to the Swiss bank account of my blackmailer.

I think about what Tara Harker told me. If the police are looking into me, they'll probably track down my mother at some point. Or my creepy boss. If they find out about my past, it won't look good. In both instances, I had good reasons for my actions. But he-said, she-said situations are risky, and somehow women always end up being tainted, no matter the circumstances.

Plus, even if they can't prove I conspired with Kyle, they

might want to try and pin his disappearance on me, especially if someone finds out I thought he was cheating. I should probably tell Roger all of this. What Tara found out. What Carla knows. He's my attorney, and you're not supposed to keep anything from your attorney. But the truth is, he's in my corner right now, and I like that he respects me and he believes me. I'd hate to lose that. Attorneys have to defend you, whether they believe you or not. Speaking from experience, though, I know it goes a lot better for the defendant when they do.

The more I think about it, the more I realize that fleeing might be my best option. But Kyle's policy is only for two million dollars. And I'll need money to get a new identity and start a new life. So, who do I pay and who do I screw over? Who's the bigger threat? My money's on Wes Walker. If I leave the country, Eddie's hold over me evaporates. Plus, my husband owes money to Walker for the project, so it won't raise a red flag if I pay him back.

"The winters there are too harsh. The Caymans, Roger. I'll put my money in the Caymans." I smile.

"Very funny, Morgan."

"Don't worry, Roger. I get your point. Is there anything else?"

"Yes," he says. And he proceeds to go over a new case with me. A tax situation. Nice and boring, but perfect for me. I like numbers and this is the kind of challenge I enjoy. He needs me to do research on how to get his client a deal with the IRS.

He heads for the door after we're done. As he's exiting, I call out to him.

"Roger?"

"Yes, Morgan?"

"Thanks. For everything. I don't have a lot of people I can count on in my life. You're a good friend."

He beams, and I think he's blushing a little. "It's nothing, Morgan," he says.

But I see a mile-wide grin on his face as he walks away.

"IS WES WALKER IN?" I ask.

It's the same receptionist from the last time.

"Do you have an appointment?"

"No," I say.

"And you are?"

Does she seriously not remember me, or is this some kind of scripted protocol she's required to recite? How could you not remember someone whose face has been plastered all over the news in the most sensational missing persons case to hit the Bay Area in nearly a decade?

"Morgan Murphy," I remind her.

"Right," she says, as if she remembers me now, like I'm someone she met at a cocktail party, not a potential suspect in a police investigation. "Take a seat, and I'll see if he's available."

After ten minutes or so, she sends me in.

"Morgan Murphy. To what do I owe the pleasure?" Walker asks.

"I thought it was time I get back to you with an answer," I reply.

"And what did you decide? Please, take a seat."

I'm still standing, because I planned to make this quick. But I decide it's best to oblige. He seems harmless on the surface, but there's a look deep in his eyes that tells me he's not the type of man who likes to be disappointed or rushed.

Clearing my throat, I take a seat. "I've decided it's best for me to pay you back and wash my hands of the project. It's nothing personal. It's just that I've got too much on my mind right now. It's not the right time."

"I appreciate your honesty and your position."

I take a deep breath. "I'm working on getting the funds to pay you back for your investment in the project."

"And what will you do then?"

"I'm not sure. Cancel the construction loan. Sell the land. Pay back the smaller investors."

"I don't understand something, Morgan. Why come to me now? Why not wait until you sell?"

"Huh?" I ask.

And then my stomach sinks.

Because I see what he's getting at. "You're by far the biggest investor. I didn't want you to worry that you wouldn't get your money back."

"But I already told you that I wasn't worried about that."

I look away, knowing that I've just backed myself into a dangerous corner. I'm sure he knows that I suspect that he might be a threat to me.

"Morgan. Let me ask you something. And I'm going to need you to be honest with me. When you were at your old firm, did you, perhaps, hear some unflattering things about me? And my timber business?"

I sigh, realizing that I don't have much choice but to come clean about it. "Yes, Wes. I heard some rumors."

He punches his desk. So hard that he's now rubbing his fist and twisting his wrist, like he's afraid he broke it. "That son of a bitch! He's always had it in for me."

"Who's always had it in for you?"

"Your former boss. I always suspected he started it, but I never knew for sure."

"My former...you mean Larry Maddox?"

My stomach turns at the mention of his name.

"Exactly," he says. "We've got a rivalry that goes back a few decades. And I can assure you, my business is on the up and up. This whole federal crackdown is bullshit, too. People are buying tech devices and running shoes and bathing suits that are made in sweatshops, and that's just fine. But if I happen to import a piece of ebony that was misrepresented in a complex supply chain that might disrupt the habitat of some butterfly that nobody's heard of, I'm a criminal? I'm doing the best I can in a tough business, Morgan. And people want what they want. Someone's going to give it to them. But I've never knowingly broken the law."

I'm only half listening to him, because bile is rising in my throat. "I...I'm sorry, Wes. I didn't mean to upset you."

"No, no, darlin'. I'm not upset with you." Walker's face takes on a look of concern. He squints, honing in on my face. "You don't look too good, sweetheart. I didn't mean to frighten you. Do you need some water?"

I shake my head. "No, thanks. I'm fine. You didn't frighten me. It's just, hearing the name of my former boss makes me sick to my stomach."

A grin starts to form on his face and he lets out a chuckle. "Oh, really? Tell me more, Morgan. Because I heard a rumor about you, too. That you might perhaps have some dirt on your former boss. Whose name I won't mention, of course, in light of your condition."

Based on Walker's rant, I'm guessing he's full of shit. Even if he's not in bed with any drug cartels, I'm sure he's turned a blind eye a few times. But I don't care. It's not my problem. All I need to do is make sure he's not after me. And now that we have a common enemy, I've pretty much sealed the deal. But I'm not at the point yet where I want to pull the trigger and use my dirt. I don't need another enemy coming after me. I need time to think.

"Nothing like that, I'm afraid. He's just your garden variety creep. And an asshole to work for. But something positive came out of my time there. Kyle was a client, and I met him there. Which brings me back to the point of my visit. I'll have your money in two weeks or so. Is that soon enough?"

"Absolutely. Let me know before you put the land on the market. I might want to make you an offer before you sign a listing agreement. I love a good deal."

"Will do," I say. "And I need to get going now."

We say our goodbyes, and I stand up to leave. But as I'm turning towards the door, he calls out to me.

"Morgan? One last thing."

"Yes, Wes?"

"If you did perhaps have some dirt on that jackass, and you wanted to let me use it to get back at him, I'd be forever in your debt."

I nod. "Good to know."

Having a guy like Wes Walker forever in my debt is a tempting proposition. And so is getting back at Larry Maddox. But as I said, I don't need another enemy. And now I've got a tough decision to make.

But that's a good problem to have.

TWENTY-THREE
MORGAN

Hunger overtakes me the minute I get into the house, which is a positive sign. I haven't had much of an appetite lately, but the progress I've made over the last few days gives me hope. I finally feel like I'm getting ahead of this. And I'm not going to lie. The thought of getting back at Larry Maddox makes me smile. Even if I don't do it, I like the thought of having even more power over him.

Our kitchen is spotless, which is one perk of being husbandless. Kyle's not a slob, but his standards for cleanliness are much lower than mine. Stir-fry sounds good. I've got shrimp, broccoli, and onion, so I get to it. Soon it's sizzling in the pan, and I can smell the garlic and basil. I steam some brown rice in a bag. A glass of wine would be nice. A chance to finally relax and take a beat.

I settle in at the dining table and start to eat, stuffing down the feeling of loneliness that hovers just below the surface, reflecting on all I've accomplished in the last few days, feeling a sense of satisfaction. I eat fast, and I must say it's delicious. Kyle liked heartier fare, and we have different tastes. I'd eat like this every night if it were up to me. I'm almost done when I hear a knock at the back door. It startles me, and Roger's warning rings in my ear.

I scarf down the remaining forkfuls of my pungent dish and take a last long sip of my crisp Pinot Grigio. If it's the police coming with an arrest warrant, this might be my last meal. I'm sure the food in county jail is positively awful, and I'm certain there's no wine. Maybe in state prison there is, if you can work your way up the hierarchy or bribe a guard. But not in county jail.

Peeking out the window, I'm in a momentary state of shock.

Carla?

What on earth is she doing here?

"Morgan!" she calls out to me in a forceful whisper. "Are you in there?"

I rush over and open the door, thankful for the fact that I won't be leaving tonight in handcuffs. "What do you—"

"Let me in! I don't have much time."

Her husband is trying to blackmail me. She's been ignoring my calls. I'm pretty sure she was wearing a wire the last time she was here. I should probably slam the door in her face.

But I don't.

Because I know she's taking a risk coming here, and my heart melts. I hadn't realized how sad I was at the thought of losing the one friend I have, and at the idea that she betrayed me. I can see by the look in her eyes that she hasn't.

I pull her in and shut the door. "What's going on?" I ask.

Her index finger flies towards the window. "Close the

curtains! We don't have much time. And I have a lot to explain."

My brain struggles to process what's happening. I close the curtains, but I'm not moving fast enough for her. She's already seated at my dining table.

Her eyes widen. "Come here! Sit!" she commands. "I only have a few minutes."

I obey, not taking my eyes off of her as I place my hands on the tabletop and make a slow descent into my seat, still reeling from the fact that she's sitting at my table.

"I'm sorry about Eddie," she says. "I just found out what he did. That wasn't my idea, Morgan. And he's not doing this to be an asshole. He's terrified. He wants us to move to the Philippines!"

"What? Why?"

"The police came to me the day after Kyle went missing. They made me wear a wire that time at your house."

"I knew it."

She shrugs. "I figured you'd catch on. It's not like I could tell you. Then they tried to flip me, but I wouldn't budge. I stuck to our story. But Eddie's got a bad feeling about this. He found the photos on my phone of the brunette woman. He keeps saying that you might have done it. And he doesn't trust the guys either, now that they're demanding money. He's afraid they might never stop. He wanted me to come clean and make a deal with the cops. But I won't do that. Not just because of you, but because of my kids. The police will promise the world, but you never know what they'll really do once you tell them what they want to hear. I can't end up in prison. So, Eddie decided to come after you about the money. And then he wants to leave and start over."

Something crosses my mind.

"Carla?" I ask.

"Yes?"

"How well does Eddie know the guys we hired?"

"I'm not sure. Why?"

"Do you think they could have done this? Took Kyle and killed him? Now that they're blackmailing me, it seems possible. And Kyle's car was found in Sunnyvale."

She pauses. "I don't know, Morgan. They didn't know about your life insurance."

"Most people have life insurance, Carla. Everyone knows that."

"Anything's possible, I guess."

"Maybe we could use this. Flip it back on them. Tell them we figured it out and threaten to go to the police."

"Right. And if they are actually murderers, then we're next on their hit list."

"That's a fair point."

And I'm starting to see why Eddie's so mad at me.

This is all my fault.

Me and my bad temper.

"I have to go," she says. "The best thing for all of us is to get that insurance money and pay them off. Once we have proof of the shakedown, it'll be harder for them to go to the police if they double-cross us. Watch out for the cops, too, Morgan. They're not on your side."

I explain to her about going to the police, and Detective Rodman and the provisional death certificate. And that I need to get word to Eddie that the money's coming but it might be a few weeks. "Can you find a way to tell him?" I ask.

She looks off in the distance, and then back to me. "Come to my office tomorrow. Make up some reason to stop in. And then come over and whisper something to me, so I can sell this to Eddie. I'm not a great liar, and we need to make it believable. Plus, then there will be witnesses."

I nod. "Good plan. Any chance you could get Eddie to come down a little on that demand?"

"Make him an offer, and I'll see what I can do. Once he tells me about it. Now, I really need to get out of here."

She stands, turns from me, and heads for the door.

I follow her. "Carla?" I say.

She turns around. "Yes, Morgan?"

"Thank you." I reach out and hug her tight against me. She hugs me back, and it gives me strength, knowing I still have a real friend in this crazy world.

She pushes back from me and looks me in the eye, her hands planted firmly on my shoulders. "One more thing. That reporter's been hounding me for an interview. I think she's finally given up. But watch your back with her, too."

Damn that Tara Harker.

And then she's gone.

TWENTY-FOUR
MORGAN

I enter Kyle's workplace looking for Carla, after the receptionist gives me her blessing. I needed to come here anyway, to clean out Kyle's desk and take care of some paperwork. It's mid-morning, and I don't see her at her desk. There's a buzz in the air, and a woman in a fitted white dress with red pumps does a double-take when she catches me looking towards her. I expected a little more sympathy, frankly. It feels like I'm being judged.

Heading into Kyle's office with my empty box, I start to pack up his things. A photo of the two of us sits on his desk. It's a nice photo. Nothing special. The two of us sitting in our back patio, and somehow that makes me sadder than if it had been one of our exciting trips, to Paris or Buenos Aires, or Kauai. Because it's the everyday life I miss. I wonder if that's why he selected this photo, if those were the memories he treasured the most. And I think, again, that I might have it all wrong. Maybe he wasn't cheating.

But then I remember the perfume, and it seems as if I'm

kidding myself. Both things could be true. He could love me. Love our life together. And he could still have been cheating. I start throwing his things in the box, all the while keeping an eye out for Carla, itching to get out of here. Something about the energy around here is making me nervous.

"Morgan," Carla whispers from the doorway. "Come here." She waves me over.

I rush over. "What is it?"

"You didn't hear this from me, but there's something hinky going on with the books."

"Hinky?"

"There are some financial irregularities. And some of it seems to be pointing back to Kyle. That's all I know. And you need to promise not to say anything."

Irregularities?

What does that mean?

"I...um. What should I do?"

"Nothing, for now. Play dumb. I need to go."

Play dumb? I don't have to play, because I have no idea what's going on. Did Kyle embezzle or something?

But I do as I'm told. And when I meet with HR, I play the role of grieving wife. Some woman named Dorothy gives me the figures on his next commission and when it will hit our checking account. He's not an employee, she says, so there's no sick or vacation time coming. His health insurance is through me, I say, and she mentions that at some point, I might want to cancel it. She winces as soon as the words leave her mouth.

"I'm sorry," she says. "That was insensitive."

"It's fine," I reply.

This Dorothy woman seems to have no idea about this

financial irregularity situation brewing outside her door. Or if she does, she's not letting on about it to me. It can't be that bad if they're giving me his last commission, can it?

But I leave with a vengeance, knowing what my next move will be. The walls are closing in on me, and I might not have much longer to make my move.

LARRY MADDOX WAS A VILE MAN. I could see that right from the start. But he wasn't the kind of guy whose personality snuck up on you. You knew who he was from the minute you met him, I must give him that. But I needed a job, and he gave me one when I finished my paralegal program. A pretty good job. I knew he had a reputation for flirting, and I was sure it went further than that. You hear things, and as I said, he wasn't trying to pull anything over on anyone.

I brushed off his flirtations for the first year. He's in his sixties now, so he's not *that* old. Not old enough to excuse his behavior. By the time I met him, he'd worked for decades in a world where women were supposed to be equals. Treated with respect. But clearly, he didn't get the memo, or perhaps he didn't care. He was married, and his wife held the purse strings. He had partner-lawyer money, but she had old money. Lots of it. Perhaps that's why he asserted his dominance over women in the workplace. He couldn't do it at home.

After what happened with my stepfather, I made it my business to learn to defend myself. I took classes. I'm small, but I learned one thing that was very important. You need to fight back. Most of them don't expect it. And if you come on strong, chances are they'll back off. Of course, if someone has a gun or a knife, that's a different story. But I figured that was unlikely to happen.

One night at our Christmas party, he asked me to accompany him into his office to talk about my Christmas bonus and a promotion he wanted to offer me. I told him I didn't want to, but he wouldn't take no for an answer. So, I followed him, thinking that the worst he might do is try to plant a sloppy kiss on me. I didn't think he'd try anything more with everyone milling around outside his door.

Once we got into his office, I realized that the music was louder than I thought. He locked the door behind us. Someone might not hear me scream, and I started to think I'd made a big mistake.

He sauntered to his minibar, set two crystal glasses in his palm, and plopped a few ice cubes in them. Then he poured some scotch in each of them and handed one of the glasses to me. Rather than drink it, I placed it on the counter and folded my arms.

"So, what did you want to talk to me about, Larry?" I asked.

"Don't play coy with me, Morgan. You know why we're here."

"Yes," I said. "To talk about a raise."

"If that's what you kids are calling it." He smiled.

He wasn't totally repulsive looking or anything. A decent-looking older guy. But he smelled of stale sweat and garlic breath mixed with scotch. Plus, I don't like older men, especially ones who force themselves on younger women and won't take no for an answer. He reached for me, and I told him to back off, thinking that if I came on strong, he might back down. Fire me, maybe. But back down.

But he didn't.

He grabbed me and pulled me to him, attempting to kiss me on the lips. I shoved him forward and kneed him in the balls. That might have been the end of it, but he got a crazed look in his eyes, like he was going to come after me.

"You bitch! I'll ruin you." He lunged at me.

In an instant, I grabbed his wrist, spun him around, and pulled his arm behind his back, shoving it up towards his shoulder. He screamed out in pain, and I worried that someone would hear him.

"Quit being such a baby," I said.

Then I took out my equipment, but he couldn't see it because his back was to me. Most women don't carry rope and zip ties in their handbags, but I'd been expecting this. I secured one of the ropes around him while he was still reeling from my blow. Forcing him to sit, I pulled up on his arm again. Then I tied him to the chair and zip-tied his feet to its legs. If I hadn't kneed him in the groin, he would have been able to fight me off. I got lucky. This could have gone another way.

Then I pulled out a knife. Not the same knife I used on my stepfather. More like a switchblade. I cut a small slit in my forearm, just in case someone came in, so I could claim it was self-defense. That seemed to freak him out more than anything. The fact that I would slice my own flesh. He couldn't take his eyes off my arm as the blood dripped down from the gash and onto the beige carpet. It wasn't very deep, but it would do the trick if it came to that.

"What do you want, Morgan?" His voice was shaky now,

his pupils the size of small olives. "We're going to make a video, Larry. You're going to tell everyone what a horrible human being you are. You're going to apologize. And you're going to promise to never, ever force yourself on another human being again."

"And if I don't?"

"I'll slit your throat." I smiled.

I wouldn't have, by the way.

And I'm pretty sure he knew that. But he was still scared shitless, I could tell.

"What are you planning to do with the video?" he asked.

"I'll keep it to myself. Provided you never do this to another woman. But if I hear even a hint of a rumor about you doing anything like this to someone else, I'll unleash it to the world."

So, we made a video.

And I kept my word.

Until now.

I've never had a reason to use it. He left me alone for the rest of the time I worked there, although there were suspicions buzzing around the office that something bad had happened to me. We explained the blood on the carpet by claiming I'd gotten a nosebleed, and that's what we were doing in his office. Good thing he had ice in that minibar of his.

HR interviewed me, and I assured them there was nothing more to it. His entire attitude changed after that night, though, so people probably figured that there was, indeed, a lot more to it. I'm not surprised that Wes Walker heard a rumor about me.

I didn't want money. Blackmail is illegal. I wanted to

make him squirm. And make sure he never did it again. Plus, I liked the idea of him worrying about that video until the day he took his last breath. But Wes Walker is a good man to have on my side. He said he'd owe me one if I gave him dirt on Larry Maddox.

And I've got the perfect way for him to pay me back.

It's been a week since I filed for the provisional death certificate, and today it finally came. I filed the insurance claim. *Post-haste.*

My meeting with Wes Walker yesterday went splendidly. I told him what I wanted. He seemed like the kind of guy who could pull off what I need, and I was right. He assured me he'd have it all inside of a week.

A new identity.

A new life.

I need to disappear without a trace. Sooner or later, the police will figure out what Carla and I were really up to. And now that I know Kyle is in some kind of trouble at work, I don't want to risk sticking around. Plus, whoever took Kyle is still out there, and I highly doubt it was Wes Walker. It could be someone even more dangerous.

I'd never shown that video to anyone since the day I made it. And I was very nervous, thinking how it might make Walker feel about me. He said he liked strong women. But that strong? Strong enough to tie someone to a chair and slice through their own flesh? I told him what led up to it. I told him everything. He was most impressed by the fact that I cut myself.

"That was good thinking, Morgan. I always knew you were a smart lady. But you've got guts, too. And that's hard to find in a person."

And then I played it for him. At first, he looked mesmerized. His eyes widened and his mouth hung open. And when it ended, he started to belly laugh. I wasn't sure if that was a good thing. Then it morphed into a slightly maniacal laugh, and I figured he was probably reveling in the thought of what he could do to Larry Maddox with the video.

He shook his head. "You are a piece of work, little lady. I'm impressed. And I'm not easy to impress. You've done the world a great service."

"You think so?"

"I have a daughter. Of course I think so. I'm surprised your papa didn't rip his beating heart right out of his chest. That's what I would do, if someone did something like that to my little girl. Did you tell him?"

I shook my head. "No. He died when I was seven."

"Oh, that's tough. I'm sorry. Were you two close?"

"Very," I say.

"How about your husband? Did he know about this?"

"He knew some of it, but not all of it. He didn't know about the video, but he knew about the come-on. Truthfully, Kyle has a temper. I worried that he might do something rash and end up in prison if I told him the whole story. Plus, I can take care of myself."

"Well, I guess. So. You're telling me that nobody knows about this video but the two of us and Larry Maddox?"

"Yes."

"I won't use it until you're safely...where ever it is you plan to go." He holds up a hand and waves it around. "And don't tell me, Morgan. The less I know, the better."

He must really hate Larry Maddox, even more than I do. Because what happened next surprised the hell out of me. He offered to take fifty cents on the dollar on his investment if I signed over the land to him. There's a mortgage on it, but he said that was fine. He had a plan for using it and it wouldn't require rezoning. Something about a fast-growing tree crop.

This is a godsend, because it leaves me with more money, which I need to pull off my disappearing act. I still have a lot to learn about offshore accounts and how to handle all the transfers, but I have time. Not a lot of time, but some time to figure that out.

And then he did something even more unexpected.

"You know, Morgan. Once you do this, you'll look guilty as hell. And in today's world, it's possible that the authorities will catch up with you at some point, even if you do everything right."

I swallowed. "I know," I say. "But there's nothing for me here, anyway, with Kyle gone. It's a chance I'm willing to take."

"I'm going to give you a get-out-of-jail-free card," he said.

He wrote a name on a piece of paper.

"Memorize it," he said.

Reading between the lines, I gather that this guy is either muscling in on his territory or forcing him to do things he doesn't want to do. He said I could use it to make a deal, if it ever came to that. And if my information resulted in this guy getting out of the timber supply chain, he'd be eternally grateful.

I have no idea why he doesn't simply go to the feds himself, if he wants to get this guy out of the way. That probably means Walker is doing something illegal, or this guy is too dangerous to turn in. But I wasn't about to ask any questions. He's been good to me, but I get the feeling Walker's not as harmless as he'd like me to think he is.

Then he told me to sit tight. That he'd get back to me when he had my documents. And in the meantime, I'm to work on getting him the land and the half a million. I've got an attorney at work who can handle the title change, one of the benefits of working at a law firm. And that won't raise any red flags. Everyone knows that I'm in the hole because of Kyle's project and that I need to pay back his investors.

Today is Saturday, and I'm about to get on the issue of offshore accounts when Tara Harker calls. I let out a sigh. But I don't want to piss her off. I'm so close to getting out of here, and I need to keep her placated until I do.

I pick up, and she asks me to meet with her. We go back and forth, but eventually we land on three o'clock this afternoon. Tara Harker's become a curiosity to me, as I'm sure I have to her.

And I have to admit, I'm looking forward to seeing what she has to share with me.

TWENTY-SIX

TARA

"Thanks for the tea," I say.

"You're welcome," Morgan replies.

I'm dressed in jeans and a tan sweater, trying to look casual. No cameraman. No notepad. Hoping that I'll get her to open up to me. This time, I accepted her offer of refreshments, and we're both drinking iced tea. I take a sip of my cool drink and place it on the coaster, which sits on her glass coffee table. Then I sit back on the sofa and cross my legs. Morgan's across from me, in an armchair, wearing a navy cotton dress that brings out the blue in her eyes.

So far, it's been awkward, and we both suffer through this uncomfortable, prolonged silence. I'm not leaving without some answers, though.

Her home is spotless, and I wonder if it's always like that or if she cleans up for me. "That's a lovely bowl," I say, pointing to an elegant crystal Waterford that sits at the center of the table. It has a blue hue that reflects off the table-top, adding a splash of color to the otherwise minimalist off-white decor. Maybe it will get her talking and she'll tell me a story about it.

"Thanks," she says. "So, what can I do for you, Tara? Why are you here? Have you found anything out about Kyle's case?"

So much for small talk.

"I wanted to talk about your past. And to warn you. I want to help."

She rolls her eyes. "I don't need your help, Tara. And you've already warned me."

"Your mother said she wouldn't go to the police unless they came to her first. But she seemed to feel guilty that she hadn't. She thinks you may have done something to Kyle. And I think the guilt might break her. But if there was a reason you did something to your stepfather? Then she would understand."

"Why do you care, Tara? Why are you here with me, on a Saturday afternoon, instead of out there, living your life?"

It's a fair question.

"Work is my life, Morgan."

"And how's that working out for you?"

"This isn't about me."

"Isn't it?" she says. "How is it, being married to your job? You're not married. Ever come close?"

"Not really. I've never been one to fantasize about my perfect wedding. I don't need a gravy boat or a silver platter or a flowy white dress."

"Gravy boat?"

"You know, all those silly presents you get. All that frivolous tradition. It's never interested me. I've always loved to travel. The honeymoon held more appeal, frankly."

"I didn't get any gravy boats. I did get that crystal bowl you like, though." Morgan smirks.

We both glance over at it. She's got a sharp sense of humor, unlike Clarissa Moreland. Maybe they're not so similar after all.

"It's a nice bowl, I'll give you that. But marriage has never been a goal of mine. I've wanted to be a journalist since high school. I guess we're different that way. I chose to focus on my career."

I'm trying to ruffle her feathers a bit, because when people get angry, they let their guard down and, sometimes, they let things slip.

Morgan's eyes narrow on me. "Are you saying I don't have a career? I'm a paralegal. That's a career."

"Well, yes, but it seems like your marriage was...important to you. More important than your career."

"Lots of career women have spouses, Tara. You're a beautiful woman. But you seem lonely to me. When's the last time you had a date? There's something you're not telling me about you and why you're so obsessed with me. And if you want me to open up to you, then level with me. Why are you here on a Saturday afternoon, instead of home with some significant other?"

"You remind me of someone I knew in high school," I confess.

"Ahh, well now we're getting somewhere. And what happened to her?"

"She killed herself. Because of a guy."

Morgan nods. "Wow. That's heavy. And it somewhat explains your fear of commitment. Don't worry, Tara. I'm not suicidal. But I still don't see the connection to me and my situation."

This conversation is going in the wrong direction, and I need to get it back on track, so I pivot. "Did your stepfather do something to deserve what he got?" I ask.

She sighs, but it's more a sigh of resignation rather than a sigh of exasperation. I'm getting somewhere. I keep my eyes trained on her, and she looks away.

After a prolonged pause, she turns back to me and speaks. "Hypothetically speaking, let's just say that *if* a man like that were to do something...inappropriate? I'm the kind of girl who would take matters into my own hands."

"You should tell your mother, Morgan."

She rolls her eyes. "You should change careers, Tara. It seems like you want to be a therapist, not a reporter."

"Oh, no," I assure her. "Don't worry about that. I'm good at what I do. And I'll get at the truth about this case, no matter how long it takes."

Morgan's face hardens, and the smug look vanishes from her face. "And what do you think the truth is?"

I lean in and look her in the eye. "I believe that you don't know who took Kyle. But I don't believe your marriage was so hunky dory. I think you were having problems. And if you were, it'll come out at some point. And then you'll look guilty as hell. So, watch your back, Morgan. I'm not looking to stab you in it. But as I told you from the beginning, I'm after the truth."

Morgan sits back and crosses her legs. "Well, you're the reporter, Tara. So, if your gut is telling you something was going on, then run with it. Do your homework. And if you find out that

Kyle was up to something? Please, let me know. Because someone took my husband. That same person might be after me. And the more information I have, the better. But if I were you, I'd take the focus off my childhood and put it back on my husband. What was he doing in the weeks leading up to his disappearance? What did he do with the missing money? Who was he meeting with? And where is he now? The police seem to have given up, and whatever you think about my husband and our relationship, I'd give anything to know what happened to him."

So, Kyle Murphy was meeting with someone he shouldn't have been meeting with in the weeks before his disappearance, and she wants me to look into it.

It was worth the digs about the status of my love life to get that information. Maybe I am a little obsessed with her. But I'm also a journalist, and this is a hell of a story.

She's wrong about one thing, though. I'm not lonely or bored. And when I want male companionship, I've got that covered. She excuses herself to use the bathroom, and I send off a text to Sean, the muscle-bound trainer with the smoothest skin I've ever seen who works at my gym. Our schedules match up perfectly because he's rarely available during the dinner hour.

> Nine tonight. My place. Don't be late. Or else. :)

See, Morgan's not the only one with a spicy sex life.
I just prefer to keep mine to myself.

TWENTY-SEVEN
MORGAN

Everything seems to be going well.

Almost too well.

The money came in from the insurance company. I keep thinking about what Roger said, that it seemed too easy, with the police suggesting and even encouraging me to get a provisional death certificate. It's quite possible that they're building a case against me. Which is even more of a reason for me to disappear. Earlier this week, Wes Walker called to tell me that my "package" was ready. I've got it now, all set to go.

As far as what's next, I still don't have that all worked out. I'd like to leave in the next day or two. Today is Sunday. Definitely this week. I don't want to push my luck. I put in for vacation starting Monday, so nobody will miss me, at least for a few days, giving me a head start.

I'm planning to take a train to Vancouver, and go from there. I love that city, and there's a lot of surrounding area where I can blend. I don't like cold winters or rain, but you can't have everything. It doesn't need to be forever. I'll need to change my look, though, before I go. My new ID photos show me as a brunette with shorter hair.

It occurs to me that I'm giving up on the idea of ever seeing Kyle again. A feeling of loss settles in the pit of my stomach. I suppose if he surfaces, or if they find his body, it'll be big news. I'll hear about it wherever I end up. But will I ever know if he was faithful to me? I'd give anything to find out the truth.

Meanwhile, my offshore account is set to go. I've paid off Wes and signed over the land to him. Carla has an account, too, and I'm slowly moving the money, even though Roger told me not to. What choice do I have?

Something else occurs to me. A last gesture of goodwill I can do for the two people who've helped me the most during this difficult time. I log into my insurance company website and change my beneficiary designation, splitting the proceeds between Carla and Roger. Maybe they'll be clever enough to figure out a way to collect on me when I skip town. Seems a shame to let it go to waste, especially if I actually end up dead, which is always a possibility.

Roger told me not to transfer large amounts of money, so I've been sending fifty thousand a day to my numbered account, and the same amount to Carla's. Anything more might raise a red flag. Even that amount might cause a stir, but I don't have much choice. I need to move it. So far, there's four hundred thousand in each one, and I'll be able to get the rest of it transferred by the time I leave town. I've memorized the number. I think I've got it all covered.

The front doorbell rings, and I slam the computer down. It's probably Tara Harker—or the police. I peek out the curtains and I almost do a double-take.

My mother?

What on earth is my mother doing here?

She spots me, and now I can hardly pretend I'm not here.

That damn Tara Harker, I'm sure, is behind this.

"Please, Morgan. Open the door. I have to talk to you."

The minute she sees me, she crumbles before my eyes. "I'm sorry," she whispers. "I'm so, so sorry. I didn't know. I swear to you."

Her chin quivers, and soon she's sobbing into my sweater, which I just had dry cleaned. I ferry her into the living room and set her down on the sofa. She's thinner than I remember. Well, not thinner exactly, but there's a look of fragility about her. She's aged, of course. It's been nearly two decades. But she looks good, like she's clean.

"I'll get you some water," I say.

And I leave her to collect herself.

Upon my return, she's in better shape. "Is it true?" she asks. "What Tara Harker said? Did Jim...do something to you?"

"He tried, but he didn't get very far. Because I stabbed him in the thumb."

"Oh, thank God. From what she said, I thought he raped you. What did he do to you? And why didn't you tell me about it?"

I roll my eyes. "How could you *not* have known? Didn't you see the way he looked at me all the time?"

"What? No? How did he look at you?"

"Like I was a piece of meat."

My mother sighs. "I didn't see it, Morgan. I swear. Can you tell me what happened? Was it more than once? Oh, God. The thought of it just makes me sick." She stands and holds her head in her hands, as if it's about to explode.

"Sit, Mom. It was just the one time."

I explain the circumstances, and her brow furrows, like she's trying to picture it in her head. Then looks up towards the ceiling.

"Hmm..." she says.

Hmm?

What kind of mother says "hmm" after a revelation like that?

"Do you think..." she begins.

"Do I think what?" I ask.

"Never mind," she says.

I bolt up, because I have a hunch about where this is headed. "Tell me what you were going to say, Mom." My hands are on my hips.

"It's nothing."

"Tell me. Or leave. *Now.*" I point towards the front door.

She swallows. "Do you think you could have... misinterpreted what he was doing?"

"Oh my God, Mom! He groped my *breast!* There's pretty much no way to misinterpret that. Is that why you came here? To try and discredit me and make yourself feel better?"

"No. Not at all, Morgan. I believe you. I believe everything you said. I'm sorry. I suppose I'm just trying to rationalize it. But this isn't about me. It's about you. Please. Let's start again. Why didn't you tell me?"

"You don't believe me now. Why would you have believed me then?"

"I do believe you. And I know I wasn't the best mother in the world. But for God's sake. I would have backed you if Jim did anything at all to make you uncomfortable."

"He molested me, Mom! He didn't make me *uncomfortable.*"

She shakes her head. "I know. I'm sorry, Morgan. I wasn't there for you. On a lot of levels. But I loved you. I still do. You're my only child, and I'd like to see you once in a while. I've experienced loss. The kind of loss you're experiencing now. I can help you through it. Maybe we can try to... start over?"

It's a nice thought, and it's hard to admit even to myself that there's a part of me that longs for her. Longs for her touch. I think back on when I was a little girl. How she used to brush my hair and wipe the tears from my eyes if I was upset, before it all turned rotten. And even when she drank, I knew that deep down inside, she loved me.

But I'm leaving, and right now that needs to be my focus. Plus, she's bad for me. We're bad for each other. And right now, I miss my dad more than ever. I've always been a daddy's girl, and on some level, I think that might have caused some jealousy on her part. I'm not a monster, though. So, I decide to play along.

"We can try, Mom. But a little at a time. And right now, it's not a good time. I'm afraid I'm going to have to ask you to leave."

We say our goodbyes, and as we look each other in the eye, I have a feeling she knows it's for the last time.

AFTER I'M SHOWERED and ready for bed, I need something to make me feel better. I check the missing persons website to see if there's been any news, and it seems like people have lost interest in Kyle's case. I've been avoiding my social media feeds, so I hop on, hoping to boost my spirits. The two people I was engaging with haven't sent me any more messages.

And neither has anyone else.

So much for my influencer business.

Then a message pops up.

> I told you. You're not fooling me. You'll get what's coming to you. Soon.

The person must be online now, so I reply.

> Fuck off.

But they don't answer, and it seems like they logged off as soon as I hit send. Probably some psycho. Or Eddie. I shouldn't let it ruffle my feathers. Still, I double-check all the doors and the deadbolts. I should have looked into that dog. We don't even have an alarm. Then I head upstairs to bed, thinking that I should try and get out of town tomorrow, or at the latest, the day after that. There's nothing holding me here anymore.

Except for one thing. I need to know the truth about Kyle. I open my computer one more time and draft an email to Tara Harker—with a photo attached of a brunette woman exiting the Westin hotel. If anyone can get to the bottom of it, she can.

I send it off.

And now I really need to leave town.

TWENTY-EIGHT
MORGAN

I wake from a strange dream. Images flash through my mind. Tiny people with big heads and flailing hands chattering in an unfamiliar language. I'm leaving soon for a new life. That's probably what triggered the dream.

It's pitch black, and I'm on guard. It's two o'clock in the morning, and I need my sleep. But all my senses are heightened, and I wonder if something woke me, or if it's the remnants of my freaky dream. I lie in bed, dead still, listening for any sign of trouble.

There's nothing.

Something nags at me, though, and I need to check the house or I'll never get back to sleep. Why didn't I buy a gun? I've got my switchblade and pepper spray, but that's no match for the kind of person who tried to take me at the beach. Here, there's nowhere to run. I think about calling the police, but I don't want to attract attention. I picked up the packet from Wes Walker today. What if they search the house?

So, I sit up, but I don't turn on the light. First, I grab the knife and the pepper spray out of the drawer in my nightstand, closing it ever so softly. My heart is beating so fast I feel like I might pass out. I try to breathe and slow it down, but it's not working.

Placing my feet gently on the floor next to my bed, I stand. It's dark, so I head over to the window and pull back the blackout curtains. There's a full moon, so that lets in some light. Clutching the pepper spray in my left hand and the knife in my right, I check my room. Under the bed. The closet. The bathroom. It's all clear. I figure I'll go room by room, starting with the upstairs.

The guest bedrooms are next, but I feel an overwhelming sense of dread at the thought of leaving my bedroom. In here, I'm safe. My phone is with me. Perhaps I should barricade the door and sit tight until the morning light. But here, I'm trapped. And I'm an easy target.

It's probably nothing.

I throw on a pair of gym shorts with pockets under my nightshirt and tuck my phone in the front pocket. Weapons in hand, I head out. The floorboards creak, and I stop dead in my tracks. Now I have no choice but to continue. If someone's here, they heard me. I tiptoe into the guest bedroom as my palms start to sweat, repeating what I did in my room.

The closet.

Under the bed.

Nobody's here.

I'm exiting the room when the neighbor's dog starts to bark, startling me. I try to pull my foot away in time but I'm too late. The knife handle bounces off my knee and the blade plunges straight into the top of my right foot.

Crap!

Now what?

I pull it out, and blood seeps out of the crevice. The cut isn't very deep, thankfully. My knee broke the fall. I struggle to recall the last time I had a tetanus shot. I can walk, so it didn't slice any tendons. I need to clear the house first, before I tend to it. Blood drizzles rather than pours out of the wound, and it occurs to me that this might be a good thing. Perhaps they'll think someone took me, if I manage to get out of here of my own accord.

I finish checking the remaining bedroom and bath, stopping to wrap some gauze around my foot, and then I head downstairs, leaving the knife in the sink. I'll go with the pepper spray. I've learned my lesson.

The house is still. No open doors. No masked men. Just me and my vivid imagination. I'm breathing easier now, but I won't be going back to sleep any time soon. I pop in a k-cup, reminding myself that I need to clean out my wound. If that gets infected, it could be trouble for me. I have my ticket to Vancouver. But I need to wait for daylight.

Heading up to the bathroom with my coffee and pepper spray, I take one last look around my living room. I can't bring most of the items that have sentimental value. I need to leave my old life behind. My phone, with all its photos. Left behind. Wedding photos. Jewelry that might identify me in some way. All never to be seen again. A sadness washes over me, but at least my heart has stopped pounding.

I flip on the light and do a double-take when I see myself in the medicine cabinet mirror. I'm not used to seeing a brunette with short hair looking back at me, which I cut myself, by the way. I hate it, but I have to admit, I look very different. I open the medicine cabinet and get to work tending my wound. Lifting my foot into the sink, I pour peroxide into the cut. Some people say you shouldn't do that anymore, but in my experience, it works. Antibiotic ointment is next. Then I wrap it in a new sheet of gauze and tape it up.

He comes out of nowhere, placing his hand over my mouth. I grab the knife out of the sink before he wraps his arm around me. He spins me around and presses a cloth against my face. I have the knife in my hand, but I can't get out of the hold I'm in to use it on him. He's pressing my right arm hard against my side. I bend my wrist back and forth in a slicing motion, thinking that any damage I can do is better than nothing. I may have nicked him. If I did, it didn't do much damage. I'm at the wrong angle.

Whatever is on that cloth hits me, and the knife drops from my hand. I struggle to stay conscious while competing thoughts run through my mind. This person could have easily murdered me. He could have slit my throat. Whoever he is, he doesn't want me dead.

This could be good, if money is what he wants. I have a great deal of it, and I'm happy to share. Or it could be bad, if he wants information, and he'll do whatever it takes to get it out of me. In that case, it could be very, very bad.

Because some things are worse than death.

And then it all goes black.

PART 3

TWENTY-NINE
TARA

I'm up early this morning. It's Monday, just after six. I was wiped out last night. Maybe I'm coming down with something. But I can make good use of the time. Coffee in hand, I hop on my computer and start my day.

My morning immediately gets more interesting. I click on an email from Morgan Murphy, which she sent me late last night, just after eleven:

> **This woman met with my husband at least twice before he disappeared. I haven't given this information to anyone but you. If you can find out who she is, you might get closer to finding out what happened to Kyle. This was taken in front of the Westin hotel in downtown San Jose, walking distance from his office.**

Attached to the email is a snapshot of a brunette woman wearing her hair in a ponytail, leaving the hotel. She's dressed in a suit, like she's coming from work. But no brief-case. No work materials. Her hair is a little messy, which is telling.

Did Morgan think Kyle was cheating on her? This confirms my gut feeling that their marriage wasn't as great as she said it was. That time she slipped up in the interview? When she said they went on that getaway to spice up their marriage? I believe that's exactly what that weekend was for. The truth came tumbling out of her when her guard was down, as it does with many people under pressure. Every-thing makes sense now.

Except for one thing.

Why would she send this to me? It makes her look suspi-cious. Guilty, even. It makes that whole fake kidnapping story look like a lie. And if the police find out she withheld this information, that in and of itself could be a crime. Morgan must really want me to figure out who this woman is.

I need to see her in person. Read her expressions. I'll head over to her place before she leaves for work. I'm not letting her know, though. I want the element of surprise. And then I need to decide what to do with this information. As a journalist, I'm honor bound to protect my sources, so I'm not giving it to the police. Not yet. That might land me in jail.

But that's the job, right?

"MORGAN?" I call out. I rang the doorbell twice but there was no answer. The garage door is down, so I can't tell if her car is here. It's only half past seven, and I doubt she's left for work already. All the lights are out, though, so perhaps she did.

One of the curtains in the living room is open slightly. I have to cram myself behind a row of bushes to peek in. A branch catches on my slacks and snags them.

"Can I help you?" It's a man's voice, and it's not very friendly.

I turn and see a sixty-something man with a medium-size tan dog on a leash, and I realize this must look odd.

"Oh, hi! I'm a friend of Morgan's," I say, waving my hand around like a politician on a campaign tour.

He nods, then he does a double-take. "Wait. You're that Tara Harker woman. From the news," he says.

I smile, ashamed to admit that this makes me happy. "Yes," I call out to my fan. "I'm just looking—"

"Can't you people leave us in peace? *Jesus!* We're all sick of this. I'm calling the police. You can't be on her property."

"That won't be necessary," I assure him. "I was just leaving."

By this time, he's walking away, shaking his head. Once he's out of range, I march towards the back of the townhouse. *Screw him.* Let him move to a country without a free press for a while and see how he likes it.

Nothing looks out of the ordinary. They have an enclosed patio. I peek over the wall. The furniture sits perfectly in its place, as if nobody's been out here for months.

We have our big Monday morning staff meeting soon, so I need to get going. I call her cell and it goes straight to voice-mail. And then I need to leave it for later.

My head is throbbing, like I have the world's worst hangover, and my brain is fuzzy. I open my eyes and it's pitch black.

Where am I?

Why can't I see anything?

Then it all comes rushing back to me.

The man in my bathroom. The cloth on my face. My knife on the ground.

I'm alive. That's something.

Whoever took me wants me alive.

I'm blindfolded, I realize. My hands are tied behind my back, and I'm propped up on my side. A whooshing sound indicates to me that I'm inside some kind of moving vehicle. A van, maybe? Light is seeping in from somewhere, so I'm not in the trunk of a car. We're going fast, so we're probably on a highway. I can see a little through the blindfold, but not enough to figure out where we are. I have no idea how long I've been here, or where we're going.

I take inventory, trying to see if I'm injured.

My right foot.

Something smarts.

It's uncomfortable rather than painful, and it feels hotter than normal. Then I remember the knife. I did that to myself. Maybe some flesh-eating bacteria will gobble me up before whoever's behind this gets a crack at me. Now that would be ironic.

Wait.

Something's not right.

Well, yes. I've been abducted. I'm in a van, blindfolded, and at the mercy of whoever did this. But that's not what I mean. Something's not right about my reaction. I don't feel frightened or panicky. I'm floating, my mind bouncing from thought to thought, like I'm hovering over myself.

Am I dead?

But then I remember my foot. Why would I feel pain in my foot if I were dead? I play songs in my head and mouth the lyrics, to try and stimulate myself and break through the fog. I must be drugged.

Nirvana. Amy Winehouse. Carrie Underwood.

After what feels like an hour or so, my foot begins to throb. My shoulders feel tight and my arm is falling asleep. The fact that I can't move much starts to freak me out. Whatever they gave me must be wearing off. I seem to be inside some kind of box, but I kick my foot up. There's no lid on it.

This is so much worse.

I wanted to be able to think clearly, but now all I can do is stress about what kind of horror awaits me. I breathe in and out, trying to stave off a panic attack. After a few minutes, I start to calm down.

Ouch!

Something pricked me in my left calf.

A needle?

The sensation jolted me and my pulse is ticking up again. "Hello?" I call out. "Is someone in here? What do you want? I have money. I'll give you money."

No answer.

I perk up, trying to use my awakening senses to pay attention to the sounds. I need to do something, not just lie here. I try to wiggle the blindfold further up my face by scrunching up my nose, so that maybe I can see where I am. I don't know what good that would do, but it might make me feel better. But before too long, the fog returns with a vengeance. I lose interest in whatever it is I was trying to accomplish.

I surrender to the darkness.

———

PEOPLE ARE TALKING. It's faint, and I have to strain to get what they're saying. I open my eyes. The blindfold is off, and my hands are free. I'm inside a large storage case with the lid open. Boxes surround me.

Claro.

Some more mumbling that's not audible.

Por favor.

Someone's speaking Spanish.

Am I in Mexico?

Maybe they took me over the border to deliver me to some drug lord who also imports illegal timber.

The guy Wes Walker told me about?

Walker's office could have been bugged. My stomach

lurches at the thought. Walker never actually said the name out loud. He wrote it down—which means it's not out of the realm of possibility that his office could be bugged. It wasn't a Hispanic name. Even without a name, it would be clear to whoever was listening that I know something. I can't imagine who else would take me, or why.

A door slams and it's apparent to me that we're stopped somewhere. My heart pounds in my chest. Whatever they gave me has worn off, and I feel the full weight of my predicament.

I take a deep breath, thinking about how I can play this. Offer them money. Information. If all else fails, kick them in the balls and run. That won't likely do the trick, but I'm not going down without a fight. Plus, if I run, they'll probably just shoot me, which might be the better way to go. At least it would be quick.

The back door to the van swings open. A man with a dazzling smile, wearing a light blue polo shirt over tan shorts, stands before me. He looks more like a golf caddy than some drug lord's henchman.

"Hola, Ms. Murphy. Welcome to Puerto Peñero."

My mind struggles to catch up to what I'm seeing. The man looks friendly, but that means nothing. A true psycho would probably have a smile on his face while he's torturing me to death.

Then my breath catches, as someone more familiar-looking comes into my view. I'm so stunned, I feel like I might be having a stroke. My vision blurs, as if what I'm seeing is so outlandish, my mind is rejecting it.

"Babe," he says, shoving the other man out of the way. He holds up a hand. "Stay still, okay? Try not to move too much." He turns to the other guy and barks at him, like he's a subordinate. "I told you not to open it until I said so!"

"Kyle?" He looks so different. His head is shaved, and he's grown a mustache. He's not exactly tan, but he's not as pasty-white as he normally is.

But it's him.

Rather than relief, fury grips me. I want to lunge at him and scratch his eyes out. But he said not to move.

Is a bomb strapped to my body?

"It's me, babe. Sorry about all this. But don't worry. You're safe now." He's dressed in a uniform, the kind a delivery man would wear. Shorts and a brown button-down short-sleeve shirt. And I realize now that he must have been the driver of the van. So, I guess Kyle was the masked man, after all.

I sit up, still surrounded by boxes.

"Hang on a second. I need to take out the insulin pump."

Insulin pump?

"You're giving me insulin?" I shake my head, still kind of in a fog.

"No, no." He shakes his head no and laughs. Why is that funny?

He rolls up my pants leg. "But that's what it's called. The thing strapped to your leg. An insulin pump. I filled it with midazolam. It's a sedative. So you'd sleep through most of the journey. I didn't want you to be frightened. You must be thirsty. And hungry. Let's get you inside."

Kyle removes the device from my leg, and I have to admit, it was a clever idea. Then a more urgent matter comes to my attention.

"I have to go to the bathroom," I say.

"Let's go inside," Kyle says. "It's been a long drive."

Kyle helps me out of the van. In front of me is a large villa, or a small hotel. I look behind me and see that we drove down a long road that has a black metal gate at the end of it. The road leading into the grounds intersects with a circular driveway encircling a grassy, manicured front lawn. We're stopped in front of the structure.

"Wait. Did we stop somewhere on the way? I have this vague memory. Or was I dreaming?"

"Yeah. We did. It's the medication. It messes with your memory. I tried to tell you who I was, but you didn't believe me. You were pretty out of it."

"So, I've already seen you?"

That's not impossible. Kyle looks a lot different with no hair on his head.

"Yeah, babe. Like I said. The medication. It wipes out some of your memory."

We head inside, and I guzzle down a glass of ice water.

"Is this...all for us?" I ask, looking around at the massive foyer.

Kyle hands me an overnight bag. "The closest bathroom with a shower is upstairs and to the right. I'll explain later. There's a change of clothes in there. And all your other goodies. I didn't take the ones from home, of course. I need the cops to think someone kidnapped you."

"Someone *did* kidnap me," I point out.

"I've sure missed that dry sense of humor."

"What the hell is going on here, Kyle?" My hands are on my hips now.

"Get yourself freshened up. And then I'll explain everything, I promise."

I roll my eyes, but I comply. I really need to use the bathroom. I'll deal with him later. I walk towards the staircase.

"Oh, and Morgan?" I turn back to him.

"Yes?"

He smiles. "I love the hair."

I almost forgot.

I'm a brunette now.
Kyle likes brunettes?

Kyle's lying next to me, face up, staring at the ceiling. "I'm gonna go take a shower, Morgs," he says. "Want to join me?"

"No. You go. I need to relax."

I planned on drawing this out and making him wait, but it didn't go like that. When I came out of the bathroom after freshening up, I was starved, so I told Kyle to put it all on the back burner and let me get some food in my stomach.

The caddy-looking guy, whose name is Paco, served us fish tacos, which hit the spot. He seems to be some kind of underling, but I didn't catch his job description. Kyle went into the kitchen to check on our drinks, and I didn't wait for him to dig into my meal. And the weird thing is, I heard Paco call Kyle by another name. Then Kyle said something to the effect of *you don't need to call me that anymore.*

So, when Kyle came out of the kitchen with my margarita, I asked him a question. "What did he call you?"

"Huh?" Kyle replied.

"I thought I heard Paco call you by a different name. Mr.

Donnelly. And *you* said he didn't need to call you that anymore."

"Oh, yeah. That was the old alias. On my original fake ID. I used it to cross the border the first time. And I used it to go back and get you. But I have a whole new set now. And besides, we can use our real names around here. Paco doesn't care. He just forgot. How did you get those documents, by the way? I had a whole set for you, too, but as a blonde. I almost freaked out when I saw your hair. I had everything timed perfectly, including the rest stop where I knew a guy, and I didn't want to delay our escape. But then I saw you had a set that matched your new look. They're high quality. Where did you get them?"

"I'll be asking the questions, Kyle. Once I'm finished with my lunch."

Later, I told them that Carla and Eddie helped me get the documents, which is plausible. Like Kyle, Eddie is street smart, the kind of guy who "knows people." For some reason, I didn't want to let on about Wes. I don't think Kyle would like it if he thought we were too chummy. I get the feeling there was a bit of tension between the two of them.

So, we finished lunch, and then he gave me the grand tour. The place is gigantic. It must be eight thousand square feet or more. I lost count of the bedrooms. There must be at least ten. And most of them have their own bathroom. The chef's kitchen is massive and cavernous. Sounds echo off the stone and tile, in various shades of tan and ocher. State-of-the-art appliances look a little out of place with the traditional decor. The villa has three floors, although we didn't go to the upper one. Kyle said there was nothing much to see up there. It's right on the beach, too. A beautiful white sand beach that we appear to have all to ourselves.

And finally, we ended up in the master bedroom, on the second level. He closed the door. I lunged at him—out of anger, not lust. It came out of nowhere, and he was rightly shocked. I kicked him in the shins and called him all sorts of names, and he took it like a man. He let me pummel him with my fists until I tired myself out.

Then I stood there, breathing through my nose, like a bull ready to charge. "Answer me one question. And I swear to God, Kyle Murphy, if I find out you're lying to me, I'll stab you in your sleep."

"What is it, Morgs?" He appeared mildly amused. He's always liked my feisty side, and we both know my anger is all for show. I've got some good self-defense skills, but I'm no match for Kyle. He grew up a brawler.

"Did you cheat on me?"

He flashed me his sexy grin. "You hot little minx. It doesn't work for anyone else. You know that."

That was our little joke.

Kyle junior only works for Morgan.

He grabbed me and held me tight and kissed me on the lips. Then he stared deep into my eyes, with a ravenous look in his. "It's only you, Morgan. It's always been you. Since the day I laid eyes on you."

And I knew then that what he said was true. Nobody does it for Kyle like I do. And that was enough for the moment.

We came together in a frenzy of abandon, ripping off our clothes, too impatient to undress each other. Tongues and limbs and dirty talk and tender caresses and everything all at once spiraled together, until it was all too much and we both exploded. Hands entwined, staring up at the ceiling, we caught our breath for a good five minutes. I almost dozed off.

But then Kyle spoke. "Why did you think I was cheating on you?"

And then it dawned on me. Kyle knew nothing about my plan with Carla. My suspicions about the brunette mystery woman. What I'd been planning. So, I decided to keep it all to myself for the time being, until I decided if I could trust him again.

I answered him, and it wasn't a total lie. "Because you were acting so weird the weeks before you disappeared."

"I had to protect you."

"From what?"

"It's a long story. Are you ready to hear it?"

"Sure," I said.

So, Kyle told me the whole story, or at least what he thought he could tell me without putting me in jeopardy. He said he'd gotten himself into a tight spot with the development project, promising more than he could deliver, as I had thought. He couldn't charm his way into a zoning change. That's my husband. The eternal optimist. Wes Walker, he let me know, is not as friendly as he seems.

"And he's not a patient man, either," Kyle said. "He wanted his money back."

Which didn't quite fit with my impression. Wes seemed pretty patient to me. He even suggested we partner on the project. Kyle claimed he knew I'd be smart enough to figure out a way to get the insurance money and pay Wes back. All Kyle had to do was make it look like he was dead. He even paid extra for a policy with a provisional clause in it, to make it easier to collect. I informed him that Wes took fifty cents on the dollar because I signed over the land.

"Brilliant, Morgan. That's just brilliant," he said, looking over at me, giving me a nod of approval.

I didn't tell him about the offshore account. Maybe I will at some point, but not yet. But I still didn't see the urgency, and why he had to flee like that. I asked him to explain himself.

"It got worse," he told me.

"How so?"

"The feds. They came after me. Wanted me to flip on Wes, which, of course, I couldn't do. Some brunette chick had me meet her one day at a coffee shop. FBI agent. I thought it was something else. I'd been taking a little on the side at work." He shrugged. "To keep Wes off my back. But then she laid it all on me. They wanted me to flip on him. Said they'd put us in WITSEC. But I knew those bozos would get us killed. I played along right up until I left."

The brunette woman.

She's an FBI agent.

And suddenly it became clear to me why the police were so quiet. They probably thought we planned it together, and I'd lead them to Kyle.

And I bet that's what they're thinking right now.

"Why didn't you tell me all this?" I asked.

Kyle gave me the same answer. "Like I said, I wanted to protect you."

"Why couldn't we go together?"

"What? I just told you. The insurance money." He shook his head. "Your brain's still foggy from the drugs. That's why I pretended to try and take you, too. At the resort. To make it more believable that someone took me, so they didn't think I just split on everyone."

"You're saying I didn't fight you off at the resort?"

"Morgs. Come on." He shrugged again. "Look at me."

"Right." I nodded.

"First I moved the car, while you were in the shower," he said. "After I left some blood in the sink and the parking lot. Then I went back and faked that thing with you. And then I split for good."

"Why did you take me like that? At our house?"

"Like what?"

"Like *kidnap* me? Knock me out?"

"I needed to make it look like someone took you, too. That's hard to pull off when someone's tipped off in advance. Plus, if they catch me, I can let you off the hook and say I took you against your will. And we couldn't have two of us try and cross the border. We'd be more conspicuous as a couple. I needed you quiet."

I disagree.

If Kyle had gotten a message to me, I could have pulled off a fake kidnapping. But first, I would have sold the house. But I was too tired to argue the point. And he's right. Then I'd be just as culpable for this as he is.

"Seems a shame that we'll lose all that equity in our home," I said.

"We won't need it." He smiled.

"Why won't we need it?"

"I've been setting money aside for a rainy day."

That makes two of us.

"Where did you get the money?"

"Um, I invested in crypto."

I rolled my eyes, but he didn't see me. He was still staring up at the ceiling.

Crypto?

Kyle seems to me like the last person on the planet who would invest in crypto. But I didn't push the issue. Then he jumped up to go take a shower.

I'm glad he gave me an explanation for why he bailed on me. He's set us up nicely down here. And the brunette being an FBI agent? I guess that's good enough for now. But as soon as I get on the internet, I'll get a name and try to verify his claim.

For now, I lie in bed, staring up at the ceiling. I have to admit, being married to Kyle isn't boring. The man is full of surprises.

But one thing gnaws at me, so I'm treading carefully here, playing my cards close to the vest. The brunette's an FBI agent. That explains the meet-ups.

But it doesn't explain the perfume.

"What *can* you tell me?"

I'm getting sick and tired of being stonewalled. It's been like this for the last three days. So, I camped out at the police precinct at five this morning and just caught him walking in. It's nearly seven. What a lightweight.

Detective Rodman flashes me a cheeky grin. He seems to be getting a kick out of this. "Only what I already told you. I can't comment on—"

"Yeah, yeah. You can't comment on an ongoing investigation. I know. But let's get real here. Something's going on with the Kyle Murphy case. You can't keep the press away forever. I've been trying to reach Morgan Murphy for three days. Is she missing? Did you stash her away in WITSEC?"

I had a feeling from the beginning that something was fishy about this case. Things have been too quiet with the police, like they're hiding something. I don't like being stonewalled.

"If you did, just level with me and I'll go away. I have no

interest in screwing up some elaborate ruse you're all trying to pull. But I have a feeling Morgan's in danger. And if she is, I think I can help."

He stops in his tracks.

Progress.

"What makes you think she's in danger?" he asks.

So far, I haven't told a soul about the email I got from Morgan, with the photo of some woman wearing her dark hair up in a ponytail leaving the Westin hotel. Someone her husband was meeting. It seemed very strange that she would send it to me, since it seemed to imply that her husband was having an affair. That would make her look guilty, like she had something to do with his disappearance.

So why send it?

It's my ace in the hole, though, and if he's not giving up anything, then neither am I.

"No reason. Just a hunch."

"Surely you know better than to withhold information about an ongoing investigation," he says.

"So. There *is* an ongoing investigation into Morgan Murphy's disappearance? Good to know." I flash him a sly smile.

"I didn't say that."

"You can't have it both ways," I say.

"Good day, Ms. Harker." He tips his hat to me, although he's not wearing one, still wearing that cheeky grin of his—planted on one of the most attractive faces I've ever seen in my life.

"CAN I speak with Morgan Murphy's supervisor?" I ask.

A young man who looks to be in his mid-twenties with hipster glasses and a slightly crooked smile cocks his head to one side. "And you are?"

Does nobody watch the evening news anymore?

"Tara Harker. From K-PAL."

Still nothing.

"I'm a reporter. I'm on *TV*." My eyes widen.

This obviously means nothing to him.

"Oh. Sure. I'll get someone," he says, not giving me any further instructions.

I pace around the foyer. Morgan works at a mid-size law firm, which is just like I pictured it. Glass-walled offices. People overdressed by California standards. More like New York or D.C. attire buzzing around the office. It's nice, for a change.

"Candace Thompson," a tall, redheaded woman says, as she comes rushing up to me, holding out her hand. Her dress is stylish. An off-white Chanel number with a cinched waist that flatters her figure. "I'm one of the senior partners here."

The woman's name is on the wall. She didn't need to tell me that.

"Tara Harker," I say.

We shake, and her grip is even firmer than mine.

"I know. I love your work. I remember you from that missing persons case, ten years ago."

I smile. "Thank you. That means a lot to me."

That was my first exciting case, and it's been downhill ever since. Until now, that is. And although part of me would be relieved if the feds stashed the Murphys somewhere, I have to admit it would be a bit of a letdown.

Candace ushers me into a small conference room. We sit at an unremarkable round table with ergonomic-looking chairs that push too much on my lower back.

"Morgan's off today. She asked to use her remaining vacation days, sometime last week. I expect her back tomorrow."

"Oh," I say. "I've been trying to reach her. Did she say anything about where she was going?"

"She didn't. I'm sorry. Why? Is there some problem?"

And now I think that maybe I've got it wrong. Perhaps she went away somewhere. Took a few days off. My imagination is getting the better of me.

"Um, no. We were supposed to meet, that's all."

"That does seem a little strange. Let me get Roger. She works directly for him, and they're in close contact. Perhaps he can shed some light on it."

She leaves me sitting in the conference room. After ten minutes or so, a large fleshy man with an agreeable face joins me at the table.

"I'm Roger Tillerman," he says. "Morgan's boss. She didn't tell me about taking the days off. I've been trying to reach her, too. I'm also her attorney," he says. "Sort of." He shrugs.

"Sort of?" I ask.

"The police questioned Morgan a few times about her husband's disappearance. I accompanied her. You know, just in case. To be prudent. And I tried to do some damage control after her disastrous interviews. With *you*." He glares at me.

At least someone still watches the news.

"So, you saw the interviews." I smirk.

"Yes. I saw them. She didn't clear those with me, by the way. I still represent Morgan. And I'm not looking to give you any more scoops. Especially ones that could damage my client's reputation."

"I have no interest in damaging anyone's reputation. I'm out for the truth."

"Sure. Whatever you say."

"Don't you think it's odd, Roger? That the police are being so quiet?"

He perks up.

I've hit a nerve.

"I can call you Roger, can't I? Maybe we can be friends." I smile.

"Sure, Tara. I don't have a lot of friends."

"Is Morgan your friend? If she is, then help me. I have a feeling something's wrong. I'm getting nowhere with the cops. What's say we put our heads together?"

"I can't divulge anything. Attorney-client privilege."

"What if I divulge something to you?"

"It's still a one-way street."

"That's fine. I know you don't believe me, but I'm truly concerned about Morgan. She sent me an email a few nights ago. Telling me to look into this woman her husband was meeting with before he disappeared. She attached a photo to it. That's the last time I heard from her."

His eyes widen. "Can you show it to me?"

"What do I get in return?"

He leans back, crosses his arms, and eyes me. "I thought you wanted to help Morgan."

"I do want to help Morgan. And like I said, two heads are better than one. I've got other information to share, too.

But I need something from you. Even if it's just a gut feeling. Gut feelings aren't privileged, are they Roger? Because if Morgan and Kyle are pulling some kind of scam on everyone, frankly I'm not interested. But if she's truly in danger, I want to help."

"Show me the photo. And I'll give you...something." He shrugs. "That's all I can commit to."

I pull up the photo on my phone and hold it in my palm. "Does this woman look at all familiar? Do you know her?" I ask.

"Nope," he says. "Never seen her before." His teeth are clenched now, and there's a tightness in his jawline that wasn't there earlier.

"So, Roger. What do I get in return? What can you tell me?"

"I've never seen her before. Which means for some reason, my client wanted to keep that information from her attorney. Do with that what you will."

And with that, he pushes back his chair, springs up, and storms out of the conference room.

THIRTY-FOUR
TARA

"I'm here to see Detective Rodman," I say. "And file a missing persons report."

The officer stares at me blankly. Then he picks up his phone. "Rodman," he barks. "Some woman's here to see you." A short pause. "Missing person," he adds.

I waited two more days to see if Morgan Murphy would surface. She didn't, and now I'm taking action. He greets me with his dazzling movie star smile, but I'm not having it.

"What the hell is going on, Rodman?" I'm standing with my arms folded, tapping my foot on the tile floor.

"I'm not sure I follow you. And please, Ms. Harker. Keep your voice down."

Heads have turned towards us. We're standing in the foyer, and it's busier than it was the last time I was here. That's good news for me. It strengthens my position.

"You're not going to shut me up, Detective. I know something's going on. Morgan Murphy hasn't been heard from in nearly a week, and your silence on the matter is deafening."

"Let's go inside," he says, as he places a hand on my back and guides me towards the bullpen entrance. We make our way through the chaos and into a small, dank conference room. He closes the door behind us.

"Sit, please."

I don't sit.

"Don't try to tell me she went on some vacation," I say, wagging my finger at him. "Who does that when they've got a missing husband? After they've been attacked?"

"Perhaps she figured it would be safer to go into hiding. Did you ever think of that?"

"As a member of the press, I work for the public. And if there's some kind of danger lurking in our community, the public has a right to know."

"That's a very noble interpretation of your profession." He pulls at his chin, and I can't help but notice his perfectly square jaw. And his amazing bone structure. "My experience with the press hasn't always been so...beneficent."

"I think we both want the same things, really," I offer.

"And what's that?"

"To solve the mystery. To see justice served."

He eyes me with a sprinkle of amusement. "And that's all?"

"And to advance our careers, of course. A person's allowed to have self-interest."

"Ah, now we're getting somewhere. Have a seat, please." The corners of his mouth lift to a semi-smile.

I take him up on the offer.

Then his look turns more serious. "What do you want, Ms. Harker?"

"I want to know what happened to Morgan Murphy.

And why the police aren't more fired up about this. It leads me to believe that you want this case to go away. What's the status on Kyle Murphy's case? What about that ring of carjackers you talked about with Morgan Murphy? Where are you on that theory?"

"As I told Ms. Murphy a few weeks ago, they've been quiet. Which indicates I might be right. They don't normally kill people. But if Kyle Murphy fought back, then they could have gotten spooked and moved on."

"Is that on the record?" I ask.

"Sure."

"And now that Morgan Murphy is missing, you're telling me you're not the least bit suspicious that they might have staged the whole thing?"

Rodman bristles. "You're operating above your pay grade, Ms. Harker."

I lean in. "What's that supposed to mean?"

"It means some things are better left alone. If there's anything more I can tell you in the future, I promise you'll be the first to know. That's what you want, right? A scoop?"

"What I want is to know that Morgan Murphy's okay. And that you're taking her disappearance seriously. If you suspect she played me, just let me know, and I'll back off. As I said, I'm not interested in that kind of story."

"I have nothing more to tell you. And I'm afraid I need to go now. I have a meeting."

"I came here to file a report. As her friend. And I'm not leaving until I do so."

"You can't have it both ways. Are you here as her friend? Or as a member of the press?"

"I'm here as her friend," I say. "But I reserve the right to update the public on your carjacking theory."

"Fine," he says.

And then he obliges, changing his tune. He takes down all my information, like a diligent bureaucrat. "Is there anything else you want to add?" he asks.

I swallow, knowing that I'm giving up my ace in the hole. Plus, he might be pissed that I didn't tell him about this the other day.

Serves him right for stonewalling me.

"Morgan sent me an email. Late Sunday evening. With a photo of a woman her husband was meeting with in the weeks before his disappearance."

His eyes widen. "May I see it?"

"Sure," I say.

I pull it up on my phone and hold it up for him.

"Oh shit," he says. His hand goes to his forehead.

I smile.

Now we're getting somewhere.

THIRTY-FIVE
TARA

"Spill it, Rodman."

"There's nothing to spill."

"Bullshit. Who is she?"

He takes a deep breath. "Look, I'm not trying to keep you in the dark. Or shirk my duty in finding Morgan Murphy. Or her husband. But like I said, this is above your pay grade. And mine."

"Is it above *her* pay grade?"

He rolls his eyes. "Ms. Harker, I'm not at liberty to discuss this. Especially with the press."

"Why don't you call me Tara?" I say. "Then it'll feel more like a friendly chat."

"I don't discuss cases with my friends, either."

"Well, that's one thing we have in common," I say. "And I know how to keep a secret, too. You know I won't stop digging. What if I release this to the public? Tell them the truth? That Morgan Murphy sent it to me. Someone will recognize this woman. It's better for you to keep me in your inner circle. It's all going to come out if you don't."

He runs his hand through his hair. "Let's run through a hypothetical, okay?"

"Sure," I say, deciding to give him an out. Not just because he's the most beautiful man I've ever seen in real life, but because he strikes me as an upstanding guy with his back against the wall.

Detective Rodman lets out a sigh. "Let's just say that if a person was up to something illegal. And the feds knew it. Maybe the feds would go to that person. Offer them a deal to give up someone bigger. And if that person happened to vanish before the guy gave up the information, one of two things could have happened. Either the guy he was planning to turn on got wind of it and took him out. Or—"

"Or the guy cut his losses and disappeared."

Rodman nods.

"You swear you guys weren't behind this? Or the feds?" I ask.

"We're not behind it. And if the feds are, I have no knowledge of it."

"Bonkers," I say.

"You can say that again."

"So, what do you think?" I ask.

Rodman purses his lips. "Before Morgan Murphy disappeared, I thought it was possible that someone got to Kyle Murphy. But I wasn't sure. It seemed like a big coincidence that Morgan was nearly abducted in the only spot with a clear view from one of the cameras at the beach resort, but then the husband's entire abduction or struggle or whatever was off camera. It was like whoever tried to take Morgan wanted us to see it. But she seemed genuinely shaken up to me. And I didn't get the feeling she was in on it."

"Me either. And now?"

"Now I'm not so sure," he confesses. "They could have planned it together. I started to think that when she came here and got so excited about the life insurance money. We were in on that. The feds instructed the company to let her have it, so we could follow the money. Which they're on the hook for, by the way."

"Interesting." This case is getting more intriguing by the minute.

"Well, see now? You're so good at your job, I've slipped up and said too much."

"I doubt you would slip up. I'm not that good."

"Yes, you are. But so am I. And if Morgan Murphy's safety is truly what you're worried about, you can put that fear to rest," Rodman says.

"How can you be so sure?"

Rodman smirks. "There was a little blood at the scene at her home, but not much. The amount you'd put if you wanted to give the illusion of foul play but not deplete your resources. Their ring camera recorded Morgan being carried away by a masked man, who could have easily been Kyle Murphy. Again, the whole thing looked staged, like at the beach resort."

"But what about Kyle Murphy's abduction? The police reported there was a great deal of his blood found at the scene."

"We said there was a lot of blood at the scene. We said Kyle Murphy's blood was found at the scene. We didn't say that a lot of Kyle Murphy's blood was found at the scene. It's not as hard as you would think to get a hold of blood if you want to fake something like that."

I nod. "Clever. So, I gave you valuable information. You now know that Morgan Murphy had a photo of some woman meeting with her husband. How do you know she didn't off him and collect the insurance money and then fake her own disappearance? Obviously, she didn't know the woman was FBI. I'm sure she's not the kind of woman who would take it lightly if he were cheating. The guy on her ring camera could be her lover."

"Not a bad theory. Maybe you should be a detective."

"I'll stick to reporting, thanks. So, what do I get in return? I've given you a valuable tip. And I'm sitting on the story of the century."

"What if you're the first reporter I call when this story breaks? I'll give you an exclusive."

"That covers the tip," I say. "What do I get for keeping my mouth shut?"

"How about dinner?" he says.

I shrug. "That's a start."

THIRTY-SIX
MORGAN

It's been two weeks, and I'm adjusting to life here. I've always loved the beach, but the water in California is freezing cold and the shoreline is often shrouded in fog, so it's hardly worth the trip to the coast. Here it's different. A white sand beach sits outside the back door, just beyond the pool. The water is a beautiful shade of turquoise, warm and inviting. I'm sitting on a lounge chair, looking at my legs, which are, thanks to the sun, a lovely golden shade. Unlike my husband, I tan up nicely.

I want to lose the dark hair, but Kyle thinks it's too soon. And although I'm enjoying myself here, it feels more like an extended vacation. A steady dose of this will get boring. We can't venture outside the villa and our gated area for a few weeks, Kyle says, and I'm starting to feel a bit like I'm under house arrest. In fact, I haven't been outside that gate since I arrived.

Kyle is quite proficient in Spanish, which puts me a little

on guard. When did he learn this much Spanish? I took it in high school, but I'm trying to brush up. I'm learning fast, though, and he's been here a month longer than me. It's possible he could have picked it up down here. I'm doing an online course, and I'm getting better. I comprehend better than I speak, which is usually how it is when you're learning a new language. But even if that wasn't the case, I'd pretend. It's like having a superpower, if the people around here don't think I can understand them.

Here comes Kyle now, with a couple of mojitos. He's been upstairs all morning, up on the mysterious third floor. I thought there was nothing much to see up there.

It's one in the afternoon, and we've never been into day drinking, unless we're on vacation. This needs to stop at some point, but for today, I let it slide.

Kyle says something, but I don't hear him.

I pull out my earbuds.

"What?"

"How's your day going?"

"Fine."

He takes the lounger next to me, placing the glasses on the table between us. Then he adjusts the umbrella so he's not in the sun.

"So, what's next, Kyle?"

"What do you mean, what's next?" he asks.

"Well, we can't do this forever," I say.

"Why not?"

"Because it's boring," I reply. "We can't hide away for the rest of our lives. What's your plan?"

"We have everything we need here. Sun. Surf. Food. Sunsets." He places his hand on mine. "Each other."

"Sure. But what are we going to *do* every day?"

I've realized in the past two weeks that I'm the type of person who likes to be busy. I liked my job. Being a paralegal isn't like being an attorney. But in some ways it's even better. I get all the stimulation without the stress and crazy hours. And I was needed. *Valued.* Here I feel rather like an adornment.

"I felt like that at first. It's an adjustment. Give it a few weeks and see how you feel. It's better than me ending up in a federal prison. Or getting hunted down by one of the guys who works for Wes."

"Why would he hunt you down? You paid up. Well, to be more precise, I paid up."

"Guys like him don't like loose ends."

Funny. Wes didn't seem at all like he was out to get me, or Kyle.

"Why are you a loose end?"

"I can testify against him. As long as I'm alive, I'm a threat to him."

"Do you think he knows where you are?" I ask.

"Nah," he says. "How would he know?"

I take a sip of my mojito and nod. "The feds probably know we skipped out on them. They might think I was in on it."

"If it ever comes to that, I'll say you weren't."

"But I'm here. Of my own free will. I'm not a captive. If they catch us, I'm just as screwed as you are. And Mexico and the United States have an extradition treaty."

"They'll never turn us in down here. We're pumping US dollars into the economy."

"But we're stuck here. And I don't like it. I feel claustrophobic."

"It'll die down in a while. Don't worry. Let's just sit tight. And when it starts to blow over, we can venture out more. We'll need to have some work done first. A little nip and tuck." He strokes my cheek and runs his finger over the bridge of my nose. "Then we can fake out the facial recognition software. That's our biggest risk. The software's getting better, so beards and glasses won't cut it anymore. Surgery's pretty affordable down here."

"I don't want to have plastic surgery," I protest.

"Not plastic surgery. Just enough to confound the software. Don't worry. I have a guy. He knows what he's doing. We're not the only expats hiding out down here." He takes a sip of his cocktail.

"So, we just sit here? Waiting to see if someone comes to murder us or arrest us?"

"Yes. But with mojitos." He tickles me.

My foot tap-tap-taps against the lounger. He places his foot over mine and stills it. "Don't be so impatient. We'll get there. Try to enjoy yourself."

"I'm not being impatient. I'm being proactive. I don't like the fact that we're sitting ducks here. I'm bored, Kyle. And I want my blonde hair back." I let out a sigh of exasperation.

He shrugs. "You got a better idea, Morgs?"

"It just so happens I do."

"And what's that?"

"I don't want to go to prison. And I don't want to be stuck here for the foreseeable future. I think we should be more...strategic."

"How so?"

"Maybe we can try and throw them off our scent. Then we won't feel so stuck."

"Throw them off our scent? Who says they're on our scent?"

"You never know, Kyle. Just hear me out."

And he does.

THIRTY-SEVEN
TARA

My date with Rodman went well. So well, that we had another. And then another one after that. And now, I suppose we're kind of an item. It's been almost a month. Aaron's his first name, but I still call him Rodman most of the time. Keeps things from feeling too serious. He's the kind of guy who makes sense for a woman like me to date, and that makes me very uncomfortable. But I haven't bailed yet, so that's something. It seems I'm making progress, tackling my fear of commitment.

The police finally had a press conference about the Murphy case. They fessed up to the fact that Kyle Murphy is a person of interest in a federal investigation, without giving away too much detail. Then they spun it as a fake-out. Claimed that the Murphys staged the whole thing to collect the insurance money. They told everyone the Murphys got away with the payout from Kyle's policy, but not for Morgan's. I happen to know that's not quite true. It's the government that got stuck with the bill, not the insurance company. But the Murphys still made off with a good chunk of change.

Honestly, I'm a great investigative reporter. And I still don't think that Morgan Murphy was lying to me. I believe that she honestly didn't know who took Kyle. And I also think that their marriage wasn't as rosy and spicy-hot as she would have had me believe. She sent me that photo, I imagine, because she thought Kyle was cheating on her, and she wanted me to find out who the woman was.

I've tried numerous times to contact her friend Carla, to no avail. I visited with Morgan's mother one time after her disappearance, and she thanked me for reuniting them. It seems they had a short visit right before Morgan was taken, and the mother was able to apologize, which seems to have eased her burden. There's not much I can do now but wait and wonder. Perhaps I'll never know if Morgan used me.

It's going to drive me insane.

I'm working on another story now. A potential SEC violation. Not nearly as exciting as the Murphy case, but better than nothing. I've gotten nothing back from my sources so far, which is odd. So, I decide I'll check my spam folder, thinking that maybe an email bounced in there by mistake. Sometimes people answer from a different email, especially if they have sensitive information and they don't want a record of replying to my inquiry.

I glance down the row of spam messages and see the usuals: come-ons, special offers, dire warnings. But an enticing subject line catches my eye.

Things aren't always what they seem.

The address is unfamiliar, and I should probably let it go. But something tugs at me, and of course, I click on it.

I wasn't playing you.
I was kidnapped.

Another one a few days later.

I'm okay for now.
But I don't know how long that will last.

No name.
No email signature.
The public knows I was working the Murphy case. I get fake leads like this all the time. People claiming that they know something when they don't. But just to be safe, I switch this message over to my regular inbox, so I'll know if this person contacts me again. If they do, I'll tell Rodman. Maybe he can trace it.

And then I think about who else I can track down who might be able to give me some further intel on this. If Morgan contacted me, she may have contacted someone else. Provided it's not some random lunatic. It might be a waste of time, but at least it's interesting to ponder.

Yes, I'm a little obsessed with this case.

And no, I'm not going to stop.

"IS CARLA HOME?" I ask.

"No, she's at the store," he replies.

"Are you Eddie Flores?" I ask.

"Who wants to know?"

"I'm Tara Harker. From K-PAL." I didn't come to the house to talk to him, but he's better than nothing. He's about to get into his car. I head over to him.

"Oh. Right. From the TV. What do you want?"

"I want to talk about Morgan Murphy," I say.

"No comment," he says, and he tries to wave me off.

"Eddie. Please. I need more information. Carla won't talk to me. Has your wife heard from Morgan? I'm worried about her."

"I said no comment. I got nothing to say about that woman, and neither does my wife. I'm not sorry she's gone, though. She was a bad influence on my Carla."

"How so?" I ask.

"None of your business. I said, I need to go."

"Hold up," I say. "Take a look at this."

I flash him the photo of the FBI agent. Eddie's eyes land on it, and I see a spark of recognition in them. "How do you know her?" I ask.

"I don't know her," he says. "Bye, *bye* now."

He hops into his car and goes on his way.

I know he's seen the woman before. I'm not sure what this means, but I'll figure it out. Did Carla know that Morgan thought Kyle was cheating? Carla worked with Kyle. Maybe she snapped the photo. Another piece of this increasingly complex puzzle.

But where does it fit?

It's been four weeks, and I'm climbing the walls. After that damn press conference, the entire world now thinks we pulled one over on the FBI, and that we were in it together. Hopefully Carla knows better. But Roger must feel like I lied to him. This bothers me, because Kyle did this, not me. I didn't do anything wrong. But ever since that news broadcast, Kyle's been even more of a zealot about keeping us hidden away. I'm starting to feel like a prisoner.

The funny thing is, if I knew I could leave, I'd probably be just fine here. We have everything we need. But it's the thought of it. Knowing that I can't go anywhere else. That's what's driving me crazy. I haven't been off the villa grounds since I got here. At least now he's given me a computer and internet access. I told him I needed it to execute my little plan.

I need something to pass the time until we feel that it will be okay to move about more. I was thinking about how much I liked doling out relationship advice for that short time I was in the spotlight. I can't do that again, be on social media. So, I've decided to write a book. A self-help book about how to keep your relationship strong. I can publish it myself, under a pen name, if I ever finish it. At least it will give me something to do.

I sent off a few emails to Tara Harker. If anyone's going to try and hunt me down, it's her. Not because she's out to get me, but because the curiosity will kill her if she doesn't know the truth about what happened to me. Plus, I wasn't lying to her, and I want her to know that. And although I was upset with her for tracking down my mother, it did feel good to get my mom's half-assed apology and to find out she really had no idea what a creep my stepfather was.

I'm feeding Tara little bits here and there. Truth be told, I like having a connection to my past life. It's not my fault we're holed up here, and I'm starting to feel a little resentful. I need an insurance policy, too, in case this all goes to hell. Someone has to know I had nothing to do with this. And now that the world thinks I do, I can't very well go home. I wonder what Kyle would do if I actually tried to leave. I think I'm afraid to find out.

"Hey, babe," Kyle says. "Want to go for a swim?"

"Where have you been?" I ask.

"Oh, just talking to Paco."

Kyle seems to have a lot of meetings, for someone living off his crypto proceeds. But I don't comment on it. It's merely an observation.

"Sure," I say.

The water is crystal clear today. Kyle's hair is growing back, and it's more like a crewcut now. We had some fun role-playing with that last night. Sailor on shore leave and the spunky barmaid. We splash and frolic around like little kids in the glassy water, and he spins me around. We kiss, a salty one full of sea spray. It's nice, but it's not the same as it was before all this insanity happened, and I find myself longing for the past. The way we were before this all started. I'm not in control of my own destiny now, and I don't like this feeling.

After we dry off, we head inside for lunch.

It's like this every day. Breakfast. Exercise. Swim. Lunch. At least for me. Kyle periodically disappears with Paco. I have no car. No bicycle. Sure, I'm not under lock and key. But basically, I'm trapped here.

"Kyle?" I ask.

"Yes, Morgs?"

"What do the authorities actually have on you?"

"What do you mean?"

"I mean, you said they wanted you to flip on Wes. Flip on him for what? And if you had stayed and given them the information they wanted, would you have done any prison time? What were you actually being charged with?"

"What are you getting at, Morgan?"

"I'm not getting at anything. I'm merely asking for an explanation. You said that you fled when you did because the feds were closing in on you, asking you to flip on Wes. Closing in on you for what? Flip on Wes for what?"

"Morgan, I'm not being cagey with you to keep you in the dark. I'm doing it to protect you. The less you know the better. If the feds track us down, you can claim you know nothing about any of it, which is true. If I start telling you things, you'll be a party to it. Is that what you want?"

"I'm already a party to it." I hold up my palms and wave them around the room. "What I want, Kyle, is the truth."

"I just told you. It's not in your best interest to hear the truth, at least not the details."

"Okay then, tell me one thing. Whatever they have on you, what would that equate to in terms of prison time?"

"I don't know. Why are you asking?"

"You said the FBI approached you. What was the deal they wanted to make with you?"

"They wanted dirt on Wes Walker. And if I gave it to them, I'd get no prison time and they stash us in witness protection. But you better believe we're safer here. WITSEC's a joke. And we'd be in the same situation, anyway. We would have had to leave our lives either way. And we'd be stuck in some suburb of Detroit working in a strip mall. At least this way we get to do it on our own terms."

"But what did they have on you? Prison time for what?"

"I just told you."

"No, you didn't. Did you do something illegal, like Wes? Or were they just looking for you to be a witness?"

"Morgan. Stop," Kyle implores. "I just said, the less you know, the better."

"Carla said they were looking into something at work," I say.

"Yeah, I told you. I had to take a little. To keep Wes off my back."

I stop to take a bite of my hamburger, and we sit quietly for a bit. But I'm not satisfied.

"What kind of deal could you get if you didn't give up any names?"

"Huh? I don't know. Why are you asking?"

"Because quite frankly, Kyle, this is all your mess. And I don't see why I'm being held here against my will when you're the one who screwed up."

"I'm not holding you against your will. There's no locks on these gates. You can come and go as you please."

"But I can't. Because now everyone thinks I was in on this with you."

His brow furrows. "What are you suggesting, Morgan?"

"Maybe you should take one for the team, Kyle."

"What's that supposed to mean?"

"It means if you would get a couple of months in some cushy minimum security, federal facility, maybe that's what you should do. Then we could go back to our regular lives."

"Are you insane? You're asking me to turn myself in? We have a life that people only dream of. What the fuck is wrong with you, Morgan?" His jaw stiffens, and there's a steely look in his eyes, one I've never seen before, at least not directed at me.

I swallow and walk it back a bit. "Nothing is wrong with me, Kyle. And I'm not asking you to turn yourself in. Honestly, if it came to that and you decided to do it, I'd probably talk you out of it. I just wanted you to offer, that's all. It would be...gallant. You should've leveled with me in the beginning and told me what was going on before you split on me. And if you say you were trying to protect me one more time, I swear I'm going to bonk you over the head."

"You're so cute when you're mad. Come here, you little minx." He leans into me.

My hand flies out and blocks him at the chest. "No, Kyle.

You've been a naughty boy. And I'm putting you in a sexual time-out."

"Oh God, you know what that does to me. How long?"

"I'll get back to you on that." A gnawing unease settles in the pit of my stomach. Something is totally off about all of this.

He sighs. "Okay. You win. If you really want me to turn myself in, I'll do it. I thought I was doing the right thing, but maybe I wasn't. If you're *that* unhappy, go grab the phone and I'll call. Right now. But if Wes gets me knifed in prison, I'm gonna say I told you so."

"No, it's fine. I just wanted you to offer. But the time-out still holds."

We smile and go back to our burgers like all is well in the universe.

But something has shifted.

The last week has been more tense. It all started when I went out for a run. I didn't know where Kyle was, but I wanted to find out just how closely I was being monitored. So, I threw on my Nikes, a pair of running shorts, and a tank top and slipped out the back door.

I ran for about ten minutes, towards the entrance by the black metal gate, and then back towards the villa. Then I circled around the driveway. Kyle and I had done this before —jogged around the grounds. So I did that for about ten more minutes. The road leading up to the grounds is about a quarter mile long, and I figured if I went out to wherever it led, I wouldn't be able to get back in.

But then the curiosity got to me. I hadn't been beyond these gates since we arrived. So, I ran to the gate again, thinking that I'd go out on the main road and run a little farther, assuming there would be an intercom or something I could press, and then they'd let me back in. I figured I could handle whatever fallout I got from Kyle when I got back.

But then I got to the gate and grabbed the handle to turn it.

My stomach sank.

I was locked in.

He specifically said there were no locks on the gates.

Kyle was lying to me.

Again.

About two seconds later, a guy whose name I didn't know arrived on a golf cart.

"Can I help you, miss?"

"Oh, no," I said. "I'm just out for a little jog."

"You need a lift?"

"No, that's okay. The villa is right there." I pointed towards it and laughed, a nervous laugh that spilled out into the space between us and reverberated around the grounds. "I'll be fine."

"Claro." He nodded and drove away.

When I got back to the house, nothing had changed. I could still go to the beach. I could take whatever I wanted to eat or drink. Kyle said nothing to me about the incident. But although nothing had changed, from that point on, everything was different.

Or at least that's how it felt to me.

Every time I look at Kyle now, I wonder if he knows I tried to turn the handle. Or if he sent that guy after me. If he knows that *I* know I'm locked in.

I look at him and we laugh and joke like everything's normal, but there's tension simmering under the surface. I try not to think about the steely look in his eyes when I asked him to turn himself in. I went too far with that. Overplayed my hand. My only option now is to play it cool and hope he doesn't take away my computer and my internet access.

Because if he finds out what I've really been doing with it, I'm screwed.

Rodman and I made it past our one-month anniversary, which is a big deal for me. The other day, I shot him a question, just for the fun of it, out of the blue. It's the reporter in me. I love curve balls. We were talking about racquetball or something. Some kind of tournament he's in next weekend.

"Do you want kids, Aaron?" I've started calling him by his first name, although in my head he's still Rodman.

"No," he replied, without hesitation.

Cool as a cucumber.

I smiled.

"I take it from the look on your face that's the answer you were hoping for?" he said.

"Well, that's my answer. But it's not everyone's answer. I figured better to find out sooner rather than later."

"With the kind of job I have, it wouldn't be fair," he said.

"Ditto."

We're both workaholics, and I thought that would be difficult. Two workaholics trying to have a relationship. But it's perfect. He's the only man I've ever dated who doesn't care if I answer my cell phone in the middle of a dinner date. I think he'd be disappointed if I let it go to voicemail. And if he springs up after sex, grabs his computer, and checks his email, I'm right there with him.

Speaking of email, I open my computer. It's first thing in the morning and I'm alone. We don't see each other every night, which is fine with me. And just as the Murphy case was starting to fade into the background, I see another email from that same unknown address.

Kyle is starting to scare me.
He's changed.

Then another one, a few days later.

Please believe me.
I had nothing to do with this.

If there's anything I know about Morgan Murphy, it's that she always has a hidden agenda. This is too straightforward, and I wonder if the two of them are using me. Perhaps they set this up to bounce off a bunch of servers, land somewhere in the middle of Siberia, and send us all on a wild goose chase. This time, though, I answer.

Where are you?
What do you want me to do?

And this time, I'm going to tell Rodman.

"WHAT DO YOU MAKE OF IT?"

We're in a conference room at his precinct.

Rodman lets out a breath. "Hard to tell with those two. What's your gut telling you?"

"My gut is in need of calibration. Because it had been telling me that Morgan Murphy was telling the truth, and she didn't know where her husband was. But then you told me that she played me and the rest of us and took off with a million dollars."

"I didn't say that's what I thought. I said that's what our official party line was."

"And what did you think about her?"

"Hard to say. She's a tough person to read. Did you find out anything useful?"

I sigh. "She had a rough childhood. Her dad died when she was young. Her mother had a drinking problem. Her stepfather? Well, let's just say he was kind of a creep." For some reason, I don't tell Rodman about Morgan stabbing him in the hand. I don't know what holds me back. Perhaps it feels a bit like a violation of her privacy. Because then I'd have to tell him why she did it, and that doesn't feel right.

"That's tough. Who else is she close to?" he asks.

"Well, there's that friend of hers, Carla, who's been completely avoiding me."

"Her husband, Eddie, sent Morgan some threatening messages. We think he was blackmailing Morgan. Maybe Carla turned on her. I don't know. None of us could get her to cooperate. Maybe she was after the money, too."

"That's too bad. Getting screwed over by your bestie.

There's Roger, the attorney, but I seemed to know more than he did. He was offended that Morgan didn't tell him about the FBI woman. Then there's Wes Walker. The one you're supposedly all after. Did anything ever stick on that?"

"Not that I know of. And I'm not after him. That's federal. Morgan Murphy used the life insurance money to pay him back, and she signed the land over to him. That's about all I know."

"You'll get someone working on this IP address?" I ask.

"Right after I see you to your car," Rodman says.

"Why would you do that?" I ask.

"I'm a gentleman. Plus, we can't have a proper goodbye kiss right here in my office."

"Sure we can," I say. The coast is clear, so I reach over and give him a peck on the lips.

"Well, then. I guess we can."

I flash him a smug smile. "Now get that over to your tech people, Rodman. I'll see you later."

"What happened to Aaron?"

"Old habits die hard."

"So, what do we have?" I ask.

Rodman and a tech specialist named Mindy are seated in the conference room.

"She's sending these emails through a relay service, which was to be expected," Rodman says. "It's designed to mask the sender and their location."

Mindy adds, "The server's based in Berlin, but it's hosted by a company in Switzerland. Maximum privacy. Anonymous sign-ups. End-to-end encryption. No third-party access. The emails bounce to servers all over the world. I followed them back and they all led to different origin points. Minsk. Berlin. Andorra. Phuket. Manila."

"So, she's trying to mess with us? Throw us off their trail?"

"Seems like it."

I pause. "Even the last two?"

"I'm afraid so," she says.

I shake my head and let out a sigh.

Am I really this gullible?

Rodman puts a hand on my shoulder. "It's okay, Tara. Don't beat yourself up."

Perhaps it's time to get some therapy. Exorcise the guilt that's been plaguing me since Clarissa Moreland crashed her car into a tree. It's making me soft. Tainting my powers of analysis. That and the missing persons case I covered years ago. I always thought the woman was telling the truth, and I didn't go to bat for her. At least not enough. I was young, and I didn't want to rock the boat. Both incidents could be blinding me to the fact that Morgan Murphy might be a stone-cold sociopath who's playing me like a fiddle.

"Wait," Mindy says.

"What is it?"

"I may have something. Hold up. There's an IP address that repeats a few times throughout all the email batches. That's not supposed to happen."

"What could it mean?" I ask.

"With a second-rate email provider, it could be a malfunction," Rodman says.

"But you said this isn't a second-rate email provider," I say, looking over at Mindy.

"It's not." Mindy shoots Rodman a look.

He offers her an apologetic shrug.

She continues. "*Or,* she could have added a simple batch file that would disable the VPN connection for a few seconds at regular intervals. Say, every ten minutes or so, that would show up in the string," Mindy adds.

"English, please," I say.

Mindy simplifies it for me. "Morgan could have

embedded code that would show her real IP address, intentionally, but hide it from whoever she was with."

"To my knowledge, she's not a computer genius," Rodman says.

"You'd be surprised what people can do with AI these days. You don't need to be a computer genius," Mindy says. "I'm lucky I still have a job."

"You have a precise location for the repeating IP address?" Rodman asks.

Mindy nods. "Puerto Peñero. Mexico."

"We need to loop in the FBI," Rodman says. "I should've done it earlier, but I wanted our team to get some credit for this, at least between our two agencies, if we happen to get them. Plus, the FBI might not be as motivated as we are to help Morgan Murphy."

"She could still be messing with us," I point out. "Even if this IP address lands us where they actually were when she sent it, that could be part of their plan. Get the feds to launch some major operation, and by that time they've already moved on. The FBI gets egg on their face a few times and tires of them and then moves on for good."

"Once we turn it over to the FBI, it's up to them. It depends on how bad they want Kyle Murphy. Like I said, a lot of this is above my pay grade. What does your gut tell you, Tara?"

"She's in some kind of trouble," I say, hoping I don't make a complete fool of myself.

A FEW HOURS LATER, we're seated around a different conference table in Campbell, at the FBI office. A much more upscale one.

I'm here as a witness, not a reporter. Rodman filled in Special Agent in Charge Vance Williams while I sat with my hands neatly folded on the dark wood table top. He's just about finished when the door opens and another person joins us.

"Special Agent Laura Sanders," she says, and seats herself across from me. She's a brunette, and her shoulder-length hair is down today, but I recognize her immediately.

The woman from the photo Morgan sent me.

"Ms. Harker," she says, as she places her hands on the tabletop. "Thanks for coming forward with all of this." A simple platinum wedding band with three small diamonds embedded in the metal encircles her left ring finger.

I nod. "Of course."

We go over all of it one more time, and then they thank me, again.

"One more thing," I add. "Morgan sent me a photo the night before she went missing." I look at her. "A photo of you. Coming out of the Westin in downtown San Jose. She claims you met with her husband a few times."

She nods. "We know."

"Do you know who took the photo? Or why?"

"We have the photo's metadata. Yes, we know who took it. We can guess about why. And that's about all I can tell you."

I don't like to be stonewalled. If it weren't for me, this case would be cold. So, I poke at her a little. "I get the feeling that Morgan thought you were having an affair with her husband."

She laughs, and so does her superior.

"What's so funny?" I ask.

"He's not my type," she says, and she looks over at the Special Agent in Charge.

Are they a couple?

"Well, you *were* coming out of a hotel, Agent Sanders."

She narrows her eyes at me. "That's standard FBI procedure. We can't exactly tell potential informants to drop by the bureau."

"Morgan Murphy might not know that. You looked a little...tousled. In that photo she had. Maybe she got the wrong idea. Kyle Murphy's an attractive man."

She leans in. "Exactly what are you getting at?"

"I've had a feeling all along that Morgan and Kyle's marriage wasn't as blissful as she claimed. I think they were having problems. And that's why she was checking up on him because she thought he was cheating. She told me you met with her husband on several occasions. Did you do so alone?"

As I said, when people get angry, they often let things slip. But Laura Sanders doesn't seem upset. More like amused. She pulls out her wallet and holds up a photo.

"That's my wife, not that it's any of your business. Nice tactic, though, trying to ruffle my feathers. But I'm not one of your interviewees, Ms. Harker. I'm a professional. And like I said, Kyle Murphy's not my type. If you find Morgan Murphy, though, let her know. Because I don't think the woman's so innocent in all of this, and I'd hate to be next on her hit list."

"This meeting is over," her boss says.

And with that, we all disperse.

FORTY-TWO
MORGAN

I'm walking on eggshells around Kyle, and I'm starting to think I'm losing my mind. I can't tell if I'm actually in danger or if my mind is playing tricks on me. It's been nearly a week since I sent that last email to Tara Harker, and so far, nothing. A few days after I did that, Kyle told me he thought we should shut down the internet service. I asked him why and he shrugged.

"It's just a hunch," he said. "You've done enough to throw them off our trail. Anything more and they might get suspicious. It's better if we go off the grid for a while."

With no internet access, I've made progress on my self-help book. It's the only thing I have to keep me from spinning out. I hear a knock at the door. I've commandeered one of the spare rooms as my office.

Kyle pokes his head in, respecting my boundaries. "How's the writing going?"

"Fine," I say. "Come in."

I'm seated at a desk by the window that looks out to the beach. I'm surprised how soon I tired of lounging on it.

He walks over, places a firm hand on my shoulder, and stands to my side. "I think you're right about keeping ourselves on the move."

"What do you mean?" I ask, turning my head to look at him.

"I mean, I see your point. I think we should move on. Wasn't that your idea? I thought you were bored." He brushes my cheek with his knuckle. "Speaking of bored..."

It's also been a week since I put him in a sexual time-out. It's a little game we've played before. But I can't overdo it, or he'll get suspicious. I smile and play along. "Maybe tonight," I say.

"Morgan. Jeez. I'm gonna explode down there."

"We were apart for a month. You didn't explode then."

"That was different," Kyle explains. "You weren't here. You know what you do to me." His face contorts and he crouches down a bit, as if his shorts are filled with lead. "It's bad for my prostate, for Christ's sake!"

"Did you happen to bring any of our...playthings?" I ask.

He looks at me like I've lost my mind. "That wasn't exactly high on my list of priorities."

"I guess we'll have to improvise, then."

"Ooh, I like the sound of that." He smiles.

I stand and position myself inches from his body. I run my index finger up his inner thigh, teasing him. He lets out a guttural moan.

"Meet me in our bedroom before dinner," I say. "Now, leave me to my writing. I'll see you later."

I breathe a sigh of relief when he walks out the door and shuts it behind me, but my stomach is in knots.

The locked gate.

The loss of internet access.

And now?

Suggesting we change locations?

Does he know what I've done?

If so, why doesn't he confront me?

None of this makes any sense. Kyle could kill me if he wanted to. I have no weapons. He's stronger than me. He's got a posse of underlings at his disposal. And yet, in some ways, he's deferential, letting me call the shots.

Either he's trying to lull me into a false sense of security, or I'm losing my grip on reality. Maybe I have a touch of Stockholm syndrome, and I'm starting to rationalize the fact that I'm being kept here against my will. Or maybe Kyle is the same guy he's always been. Not above bending the rules. Impetuous, sure. But crazy about me, and determined to preserve our life together and protect us.

This evening, I'm going to find out.

FORTY-THREE
MORGAN

Kyle enters, and I'm dressed in a pink satin robe, the only remotely sexy attire I have at my disposal. He spies the towels I've shredded into makeshift rope, and a sly grin spreads up his face. My stomach lurches, because I don't know if this is going to be the moment he reveals that he's on to me, or the moment I find out he's not. If he lets me tie him up, that means he still trusts me.

Rather than launch into my dominant persona, I hold out one of the strands of towel, playfully running it across his chest. "I've been a naughty girl."

His brow furrows. "Huh?"

"Take off your clothes," I say. "And follow me."

We've never been heavy into this sort of thing. It was more like play acting. We have handcuffs at home, but we only used them a few times, and never on me. He lifts his shirt over his head, and I take his hand. We head towards the bed.

"Tie me up," I say, handing him the makeshift rope.

Kyle takes the rope from me and uses it to stroke the length of my body. He takes me by the wrist and positions it to the bedpost. As he wraps the rope around my wrist, I feel my heart race, but not for the right reasons. My mouth is bone dry.

This is a big risk, I know. But if he's on to me and I don't give him this option, it might be too obvious what I'm planning to do. He fumbles with the rope for a bit. Then he sits back and lets it fall to the mattress.

"Can't do it." He shakes his head. "We tried this once, remember? And I didn't like it. It's creepy. I'm not that kind of guy."

I breathe a sigh of relief, but I need to get us back on track. He's somewhat broken the spell, and I need to move this forward.

I pick up the rope. "And what kind of guy are you?" I ask. "Are you a bad guy?"

He nuzzles the crook of my neck. "You know me. I'm a *very*, very bad guy."

"You know what happens to bad guys?" I take off my robe and whip him playfully with the towel.

"No. But I can't wait to find out," he says.

With Kyle's assistance, I tie his wrists to the bedpost, periodically stopping to tease him with gentle strokes in all the right places. Then I add another layer of rope, and tug it tighter than normal.

"Hey. Watch it," he says.

I smile. "Take it like a man."

Then I stroke his inner thigh.

"Oh, that feels so good."

Once I have him secured, I sit up, move back from him,

and cross my arms over my chest. "Okay. What the hell are you trying to pull here?"

"What?" He squints, as if he's not quite sure of what he's seeing. At first, he seems to think it's part of the seduction. "I'm a bad man. You know me. I...pull stuff?" He shrugs, to the extent that he can with his wrists fastened to the bedpost.

But then I put my robe back on. "I said, what are you trying to pull here, *Kyle?*"

We never use our real names when we role-play.

"What?" He shakes his head, like his brain is struggling to catch up with his body.

"The gate, Kyle. You said it wasn't locked. But it was! I checked it one day, when I was out front, running around in circles. And then some guy in a golf cart came up and found me and asked if I needed help. Am I under surveillance?"

He lets out a sigh. "Look. It wasn't locked in the beginning. But I know how you get. I knew you were restless. And I didn't want you to leave here. Not just because of the cops or Wes or whoever he works with. It's not a safe area. Why do you think there are so many gated communities around here? Don't you watch the news at home?"

"Why do you have all these guys working for you? I know you didn't make your money in crypto. Tell me what's going on. Are they armed?"

"Yeah. Everyone around here is armed. And I already told you. The less you know, the better."

"I need more."

He sighs. "I was a little more involved with Wes and the timber stuff than I let on, okay? But you need to trust me on this. I was trying to get us back on the right track. Trying to legitimize the supply chain. Wes didn't like that I was meddling in it. And it's better you don't know any more. For your own protection."

He was trying to get the supply chain back on the right track?

I figured I'd lay all my cards on the table while I had him tied to a bedpost. "And what about the perfume?" I ask.

"Huh?"

"You came home one night. Smelling like a woman's perfume."

"Are you seriously still on that? She had me wear a wire, that FBI woman. She rigged it up on me. I guess it transferred. Morgan, look at the setup I have down here!" His hands wiggle under the strain of the rope as he attempts to wave them around the room. "If I wanted other women, I could have a harem. I risked getting caught to go back and get you myself. I didn't hire someone, because there's nobody I would trust. Someone could have taken you and held you for ransom. Think about it, Morgan. Why would I go through all that if I wasn't hopelessly, helplessly in love with you?"

He makes a good point.

This little episode has convinced me of one thing. Kyle Murphy loves me, and he'd never do anything to hurt me. He had his chance. He's had many chances, in fact, to get rid of me. I'll circle back to that comment about Wes Walker and the supply chain later, because something's not adding up. I know I took a big risk, pushing things to the brink like this, and I wouldn't recommend it. But I needed to know if our love was for real.

And now I do.

"So you're a rat, eh? You know what we do with rats around here?"

"No." He smiles. "But I'd love to find out."

It doesn't take long to get us back to where we were, and soon I'm on top of him. It finally feels natural, not forced. All my fears and suspicions and worries vanish as the tension builds, a rush of sensations pummeling me. The release comes in waves, and it's almost too much to handle. When we finish, I sit back and look him in the eye.

And the floodgates open.

TEN MINUTES LATER, all hell breaks loose. Kyle's still got one hand tied to the bedpost. We hear Paco calling out, but we can't understand what he's saying. Shots are fired. I'm pretty sure I know what's happening, although I wish I could see more. Our bedroom window faces the ocean, though, and the commotion is coming from the front.

My plan worked.

They found me.

And now I have to figure out a way to undo what I've done. I throw on my robe and put on Kyle's shorts for him.

"Stay here," I say. "It'll be safer for you that way."

"Wait. Morgan. What are you..." He shakes his head. "No! Let *me* go."

"Don't worry, Kyle," I call out. "I have a plan."

Because it all makes sense to me now.

I had it all wrong.

And I need to make it right.

FORTY-FOUR

TARA

The FBI made good on my exclusive. And I'm about to watch myself try to sell this well-crafted piece of fiction to the world.

In a stunning turn of events, Kyle and Morgan Murphy were found murdered in a villa in Puerto Peñero, Mexico, after a tip came in to the FBI from an anonymous source about their location. And I've got the exclusive for you, coming right up.

We cut to commercial break, and I sit back and wait. According to what the FBI told me, when they got to the villa, it was too late. Someone had gotten to the Murphys first. I don't believe it for a minute, but I reported what they told me to report, just the same. The broadcast returns, and I watch myself as I inform the public what I've been told to report.

*When the FBI arrived on the scene, the Murphys were
already dead. From the position of the bodies, it looks
as if Kyle Murphy threw himself over his wife's body
in a last-ditch effort to save her, but the bullets pene-
trated both bodies, killing both of them. And I'm
warning you, the images we have are graphic. Viewer
discretion is advised.*

We cut to two photos of the Murphys, hunched over
each other like a pair of wilted love birds, blood splattered all
over the wall behind them. And then it's back to me.

*There's been no further news on the perpetrators or
their motives, and the case has been turned over to the
local police in Sonora County, Mexico, for further
investigation. The FBI said the authorities in Mexico
are cooperating fully with them, and they will
continue to update the public about any new developments.*

But of course, they won't. The FBI, I'm sure, is hoping
this all fades into obscurity. I turn to Rodman, who's sitting
next to me on my living room sofa with his arm around me.
"You buying any of this crap?"

"Not really," he says. "But it's out of my hands. You got
your scoop, though. So now we're even. The lengths I have to
go through to please you. Federal investigations. Murders."
He pulls me in and kisses me on the top of my head.

"So, what do you think really happened?" I ask.

"They had information. Or he did. They made some
kind of deal. Now that everyone thinks they're dead, they'll

be in a much better position to live their lives without fear of retribution. And they don't have to hide from the FBI anymore."

"But would someone at the top be that stupid, to buy this little charade? I mean, Kyle Murphy comes off looking like a hero. Morgan keeps up her image of their perfect marriage."

Rodman waves off my concerns. "It's because you know too much. Nobody else has all the information you have. And nobody cares. Morgan told you the truth about where they were. She reached out. She trusted you. And there's a reason she did that. You helped. You did what you could."

"Are you sure? It's not impossible that she's dead. What if she is, and it's all my fault?" I ask.

"She's not. And if she is, it's certainly not your fault."

I sit up and turn towards him. "But we don't know that for sure. You can't find out? The curiosity alone is going to kill me."

He pulls me back and into his embrace. "She's alive, don't worry. You did a good thing. Chances are, Kyle was a small-time operator in the timber business, and they've gotten higher up on the food chain because of you. The Murphys are set up somewhere in small-town USA. They're fine. Now, can you put it to rest? I've got better plans for this evening."

Rodman brushes the hair back from my face and kisses me. A gentle kiss with a hint of urgency in it.

"Sure," I say. "I'll try."

But of course, I won't.

If Morgan's alive, it could mean she was in on it the entire time. And that both kidnappings were staged. I don't think so, though. Every bone in my body tells me that she didn't know where Kyle was. And that she was taken and held against her will. She sent me those coded messages intentionally, to lead me to them, I'm sure of that. She wanted to be found.

But why?

Was Kyle Murphy dangerous?

Or did she simply not trust him to protect the two of them?

She could have been sending me another message, staging the bodies to make it look like Kyle died trying to save her. Letting me know that she had it wrong. That Kyle wasn't a danger to her. That their marriage was for real. It seems like something she would do.

Or maybe I'm reading too much into all of this. Maybe I need to let this one go. I'll try, as I told Rodman. But I'm not making any promises.

"What about Wes Walker?" I ask.

"What about him?"

"Do you think he's involved in this?"

"It's not my case, Tara. I told you. That Lacey Act stuff is federal."

"Aren't you curious?"

"We've got a new homicide we're working, a carjacking ring I'm still trying to crack, a soul-crushing domestic violence situation where the wife won't press charges even after the husband beat her senseless, and a slew of burglaries in the high-income areas. The feds can worry about protecting some endangered timber. All that money they're putting into it? It's sickening." He shakes his head. "For what? I've got people to protect. Real people, who breathe and bleed and have families who love them. The feds and their bullshit timber operation can go fuck themselves. Now can we please move on?"

That did put things a bit more into perspective. Rodman's a good man. I've never seen him so impassioned. I have to admit, it's kind of hot. And if he's not concerned about the Murphys, I'll let it go for now. He makes a good point, and he's right. I see how hard he works, and how strapped they are for funds.

But still. I will wonder about Morgan Murphy. Just like I wondered about Clarissa Moreland.

Did I do the right thing?

Could I have done more?

Is Morgan alive?

Or, like Clarissa, has she moved on to another realm?

"Sorry, hon," he says. "I didn't mean to unload on you."

"Don't be sorry," I say. "That's what I'm here for. And I kinda like that side of you. All that hot passion you keep cooped up inside."

"Oh yeah?" he asks.

"Yeah."

I realize that I've grown. What Morgan said to me that day was true, and that's why it prickled me so much. I have made my career a priority, and I have no good reason for that. It's time for a change. Rodman pulls me close and kisses the top of my head again. I turn to him and our mouths meet.

And for tonight, I leave it all behind.

When I first talked Kyle into giving me the computer and the internet access, I had planned to turn Kyle in and tell the police everything, and then use the information I got from Wes Walker to get myself a deal. I was convinced he was dangerous and that he was up to no good. But when I looked into his eyes, his hands tied to the bedpost, I started to have second thoughts. He trusted me. Maybe I could forgive him. And at that point, I was glad that the authorities hadn't caught up with us.

Something still didn't add up, though. After our interlude, but before I untied him, I asked him another question. He answered, and suddenly it all made sense. I was about to tell Kyle what I'd done, but it was too late. We heard the gunshots, and I knew what was happening.

Or so I thought.

I bolted out the bedroom door, trying to formulate in my head how I could spin this. I wanted to come out first, so they didn't think it was a hostage situation. And then I planned to figure it out from there.

But then Kyle came out of nowhere. He'd broken through the restraints.

"Morgan! What are you doing? You're gonna get yourself killed!" he called out.

As soon as the words came out of his mouth, the front door burst open and some guy I'd never seen before came in shooting. He didn't look like an FBI agent or a federal marshal. More like a local.

Kyle fired off a shot or two in the man's direction as he dove in front of me, putting himself between me and the man's gunfire. He took a bullet—to the shoulder, I thought. But just then, federal marshals and a SWAT team and a whole host of others descended on the compound like a swarm of hornets.

The guy who shot Kyle was down by then. I'm not sure if it was because of Kyle, someone else, or all of the above. It was loud and confusing: the deafening sound of gunfire, people yelling, a haze of gunpower residue in the air. I was sure I was going to be killed.

"I'm okay," I called out. "I'm unarmed. Don't shoot!"

Blood gushed out of Kyle, seeping into my pink satin robe, but he was still alive. He looked up at me, barely able to speak. "That guy worked for Wes. Tell them." The words sputtered out of Kyle, and I thought they would be his last ones. Then he passed out.

"Stay with me, Kyle," I begged.

Once they saw that I didn't have a weapon and that Kyle was down, the mood shifted. They pulled me off Kyle and put me in handcuffs. Then one of the marshals tended to him until the paramedics got there. I was worried Kyle wouldn't make it. The wound was more serious than I thought. Closer to his heart.

In my state of panic, somehow, I told them a story.

All of it true.

About how Kyle skipped town because he needed to pay back his debt to Wes Walker. That he'd faked his death so I could get the life insurance money to pay him. I knew nothing about it, I told them, until Kyle took me, too. My husband faked our disappearances, I said, so he wouldn't have to testify, because he thought if Wes got paid back and Kyle didn't turn on him, we'd be safe.

When Kyle wouldn't let me leave the compound, I told them I started to get nervous. It felt as if he was holding me here against my will. Wes Walker had put ideas in my head, I explained. He made me have doubts about Kyle. And that's why I sent those messages to Tara Harker.

But then I told them I'd been dead wrong about my husband. He'd been trying to protect me—from dangers I didn't know existed. Kyle risked his life to save me, and I'll never forget the look of determination on his face when he pushed me out of harm's way.

My ace in the hole, of course, was the name Wes Walker gave me. But I didn't use it in the way I thought I would. Because the name he gave me that day? It was the same name I heard Paco call Kyle that first day I was at the villa.

Michael Donnelly.

I thought it meant that Kyle was the ringleader, and that he was more dangerous than I knew. That's why I started to get so paranoid.

But what it really meant was that Wes Walker played

me, and I explained this to the authorities. That was the name Kyle went by when he was working with Wes, and Paco knew him from back then; something Kyle told me right before we heard the gunshots. Wes probably figured that if Kyle was on the run, he'd be using that name, so if I ever got caught, I'd unwittingly put the blame back on my husband.

Even with his debt paid back, Walker was still out to get Kyle. Get him out of the way and turn me against my husband. The man who Kyle shot worked for Wes, and we'll never know for sure how he found us. But since Wes got me the fake ID, I'm assuming I somehow led him in my general direction. Someone probably tipped him off that the FBI was on its way, and he hoped to take out Kyle so he couldn't talk. He came with backup, and the whole affair was a bloodbath. I'll never get those images out of my mind.

When he was well enough, Kyle explained everything to the authorities. He'd gotten seduced by Walker and his operation, and he'd been helping Walker find new clients in exchange for some sort of finder's fee, which sounded to me like a euphemism for a kickback. Walker was relabeling illegally imported hardwood from Peru before it went through customs, using a warehouse somewhere in Chihuahua, and he was able to undercut everyone else's prices.

I'd warned Kyle about the illegal timber rumor back when Wes was a supplier. And I guess at some point, he took it to heart. He told Wes he wanted out. The feds were cracking down more, and Kyle tried to convince Wes that they could still make money even if they complied with the regulations.

But when Kyle screwed up the real estate deal, Walker started to pressure him, telling him that he needed to stay in and keep finding him clients until his debt was fully paid. When the FBI came into the picture to try and force Kyle to give up Wes, that changed everything. At that point, disappearing was the only way out. He assumed I'd be smart enough to get the life insurance and pay Wes, and then he planned to come get me. And he thought that Walker would leave it at that, since Kyle didn't turn on him. Obviously, we both misjudged him.

The FBI offered us a deal if Kyle would give up the location of the warehouse. And this time, we took the federal government up on their offer. They staged some photos so everyone would think we were dead, and since Kyle really did risk his life to save me, we made that part of the story for the public, at my insistence.

They've agreed to the location I wanted. Somewhere warm, with a beach, but in our home country. We're in a safehouse now, but they're getting us set up at our permanent location. We should move to our new residence later this month.

I can't believe that Wes Walker. Even after I gave him dirt on Larry Maddox, he couldn't let us be. I suppose if he uses that video to screw Larry Maddox to the wall, it may be the one good thing that comes out of this fiasco.

Kyle's not so innocent in all of this, either. I know my husband. He's an alpha male. And as I thought, he was up to something that he didn't tell the feds. Later, he admitted to me that he was hoping to get his own enterprise going down here, without Wes involved, using his new identity. He wanted to win and cut Walker off at the knees, and he figured Walker would never know what he was up to. Men and their pissing matches.

That's okay with me. I know who I married. We did have a talk about honesty, though. And he realizes that it would have been better if he had leveled with me from the start. We could have figured a better way out of this. One that didn't almost get both of us killed.

He's learned his lesson. From now on, we're on the straight and narrow. Kyle's still recovering, but he'll be okay. I also fessed up about my cheating suspicions, and what Carla and I had planned to do. He found our little caper idea mildly amusing, but he was insulted that I thought he would cheat. Our little weekend getaway resulted in some pretty big life changes, ones that ironically got our marriage back on track.

So, we're embarking on a new life, with a secret we hide from the world, but not from each other. No more secrets, we both agreed. We've both learned that lesson. It's exciting, but a little sad. I miss Carla. And Roger. And I know that this will haunt Tara Harker forever. It's not like she's out to get me, but I know her type. She's curious, and I expect she won't stop digging.

I want her to know that she was right about me. I didn't deceive her. She came through for me in the end, and I appreciate it. Letting the FBI know where to find me. Tracking down my mother. Getting me some closure, which has mellowed me a little. Some of that anger inside me has dissipated. She didn't do all that for the story. She did it to help, and I appreciate it. Someday, I'll find a way to let her know that I'm okay, and that I was straight with her.

Not now, though. For now, I'll focus on the future. I haven't given up on my self-help book, but I am reworking some of it, given this recent turn of events. Meanwhile, we're busy memorizing our new roles. I'm good at it. As I said, I'm a talented actress. And after all, Kyle and I love to role-play.

And it's a bonus that our story will endure. Kyle threw himself in front of gunfire for me, and that's hard to top, as far as romantic gestures are concerned. I got what I wanted.

Morgan and Kyle Murphy.

A romance for the ages.

And now we get to do it all over again.

My mother is beaming. She's been waiting for this day practically since the day I was born.

"Tara," she says. "The guests are starting to arrive. It's time to head out." I'm in the bridal suite, about to make a life-long commitment. My mother and I make our way out towards the ceremony site. It's a small wedding. No wedding party. My father meets me at the exit and takes my arm.

"Ready?" he says, with a tear in his eye, looking out at the makeshift aisle.

"Yes, Dad. Are you?"

He nods and wipes the tear away. We both smile.

I thought I'd be nervous, but I'm not. I'm excited. Not as excited as my mother, though. She put announcements of the engagement and the wedding in the local papers, like we're the Kennedys or something. But I am a local celebrity, and it did generate some press. My co-anchor likes to tease me about it as part of our repartee, the fact that I'm finally settling down.

We're getting married at a winery in Napa, and the setting is stunning. The ceremony is outdoors. In front of me is a yellow grassy lawn with rows and rows of twisty grape vines in the distance, framed by gentle rolling hills. Soft music from a harpist fills the air, a rendition of "A Thousand Years," as I make my way down the aisle. I see Rodman smile at me as he stands tall under the archway. I remind myself to call him Aaron during the vows, although I kind of like it the other way.

I haven't thought about Morgan Murphy in a while. Like I promised Rodman, I've moved on. She crosses my mind now, and I let it happen. Wes Walker was eventually charged for importing illegal timber, but nothing much came of it. He got a sizeable fine and probation, and that was that. He's got some new business he's starting up on the agricultural parcel he bought from them, so if the Murphys are alive and well, I doubt they have much to worry about from Walker.

But I still wonder about Morgan. Is she alive? Did they stay together? Does she know that Kyle wasn't cheating? I did a personal interest story on the FBI agent who worked the Murphy case, with a small segment on her personal life, thinking that if Morgan was alive, she'd finally know the truth. Kyle wasn't having an affair with the woman in the photo.

It's possible I'm here today because of Morgan, which might be the reason she's on my mind. Because if she hadn't prodded me that day and called me out on my fear of commitment, perhaps I wouldn't have been so motivated to prove her wrong.

"THERE'S ONE MORE," my mother says. "I don't know who it's from. At least I think it's a gift. Or maybe it's just a package."

Neither Rodman nor I are into gifts, so my mother and I opened most of them, but she was more excited about the whole affair than I was. Mom and I are in our living room. My husband got bored and went into the study to do some work. We haven't changed that much, and we're both still in love with our careers.

She hands me a medium-sized square cardboard box. The return address is from Lincoln, Nebraska, but there's no name on it. Inside is a smaller box with white glossy wrapping paper and a cobalt blue ribbon tied around it with a bow on top.

I unwrap the present and peek inside.

There are three items.

The first item is a book entitled *Top Ten Tips to Keep Your Relationship Strong and Healthy*. It's dog-eared at a spot towards the back, and it appears to count back from number ten to number one. I open it where the page is folded back.

TIP NUMBER ONE:
HONESTY IS THE BEST POLICY

I used to think that holding something back once in a while from my significant other was a good thing. That it added an aura of mystery to the relationship. And maybe that's true for little things, but not for the big ones.

Big secrets breed distrust, and without trust, you have nothing. You've picked this partner for a reason. Trust yourself and trust that life will be better if you let them in on what's bothering you. And if you don't trust them enough to let them in, then you need to get out. Because you can't have love without trust. Not in the long run. And the long run is what we're shooting for here, right?

I put the book aside for a later time and reach into the box again. The second item is a crystal Waterford bowl, a little smaller than the one Morgan Murphy had in her home, but similar in style.

"That's lovely," my mother says.

I place it on my coffee table.

She picks up the book and combs through it. Her eyes widen. "Oh, I've heard about this book! It's a big hit. One of the book club ladies was talking about it. And I heard the author's donating part of her royalties to some organization that helps victims of sexual abuse. Did you know that, Tara?"

"I did not."

Mom excuses herself to go to the bathroom. Then I reach down into the box and take out the third item, still wrapped in tissue paper. I unwrap it and behold the ugliest gravy boat I've ever seen.

I smile.

Then I place it back in the box and put it with the trash.

Morgan Murphy.

She had to have the last laugh.

But she trusts me, and I'll keep her secret. It was nice of her to satisfy my curiosity. And I doubt she would risk doing something like this if she had pulled one over on me; I assume that, whatever happened at the resort, she didn't know what Kyle was planning.

Mom comes back and joins me. "Did you figure out who sent that?"

"Yes, Mom. An old friend. Nobody you know."

And we leave it at that.

But of course, I'll take her advice and tell Rodman, even if he'd rather not know. Because she's right. I can't start off my marriage hiding a secret this massive from my new husband. I shake my head and smile.

Damn that Morgan Murphy.

ACKNOWLEDGMENTS

My sincere thanks to the many people who helped me craft this novel and bring it to completion. Thanks goes out once again to my husband who brainstormed with me endlessly when I hit plot challenges and who also read countless drafts of my manuscript.

Thanks to my invaluable alpha and beta readers Robin, Susan, and Donna who offered excellent suggestions and encouragement. Thanks to my chief beta reader Christina Yother whose suggestions and attention to detail went way beyond a typical beta read, offering valuable ideas to make the manuscript better. Thanks to my fabulous editor at BooksGoSocial, and to the entire team for their expert advice in marketing and promotions. Thanks to my old friend Michael Donnelly from my home town of Fair Lawn, New Jersey, who I reconnected with on Facebook. He told me that he liked my books and mentioned that his was a fabulous name for a book character, a suggestion that proved very timely. As luck would have it, I was searching for an alias for Kyle Murphy at just that point in time.

Thanks to all of my advance copy readers on NetGalley and Booksprout who take the time to read and review my books and post their thoughts. Thanks to my fellow thriller authors R.G. Belsky, Douglas Corleone, Tracey Devlyn,

Laurie Dove, Noelle W. Ihli, Leslie Lutz and Neil Turner for their support, encouragement, advice, and camaraderie. And thanks to K.L. Romo at *The Big Thrill* for promoting my new releases and to International Thriller Writers (ITW) in general. I've learned so much from my affiliation with ITW and all of its amazing members.

Finally, thanks so much to my readers. You are why I keep writing, and I am so grateful for the time you take to read my books as well as rate and review them. I read all of my reviews and it helps me to improve, so please keep them coming. I really appreciate it. I'm working on two projects at present, and hope to release one or both sometime in early 2025. For updates, book reviews and special offers, please go to www.bonnietraymore.com and sign up for my quarterly newsletter. While there, you can download a free copy of *Stark Justice: A Honolulu Cold Case*, a novelette intro to my award-winning Hudson Valley Series.

ABOUT THE AUTHOR

Bonnie Traymore is the award-winning, Amazon charts international bestselling author of seven domestic suspense thrillers. Her books feature strong but relatable female protagonists who find themselves in extraordinary circumstances. Originally from the New York City area, she's lived in Honolulu with her family for the last few decades but travels regularly. She's also an accomplished non-fiction writer, historian, and veteran educator with a doctorate in United States History. She has taught at top independent schools in Honolulu, Silicon Valley, and New York City, and she's taught history courses at Columbia University and the University of Hawai'i.

HEAD CASE: A SAMPLE

Please enjoy a sample of *Head Case: A Psychological Thriller:*

PROLOGUE

KIMI

Kimi knows what the other teachers call her behind her back. She's heard them before, although she's pretty sure they don't know she knows.

Here comes the mole.

It's not like she signed some formal agreement. And it's not like she had much of a choice. It had all started pretty innocently. Her boss befriending her and then subtly starting to pump her for information.

Then it became an unstated directive. A quick promotion to English department chair in exchange for some hints about who might be plotting behind the woman's back. Getting her preferred chaperoning duties in exchange for a few tidbits about who might be holding up her latest initiatives.

And then it became even more complicated.

She wonders how Brooke will take the resignation letter she left in her mailbox yesterday afternoon. It's a terrible career move to leave now, just two weeks before winter break. But Kimi feels that she doesn't have much choice.

It's not just the strained relationship with the other teachers, although that's part of it. It's that she's pretty sure her boss doesn't know what she overheard, and it needs to stay that way. She'll go back to North Carolina and regroup, then come back for the rest of her belongings some other time.

As she enters the deserted Cortlandt train station and starts walking towards the tracks, she feels a chill run up her spine. It's dead still on a frigid Saturday morning. No commuters. Not another passenger in sight. But she has a nagging sensation that she's not alone.

Is someone following me?

She stops for a moment and turns to look behind her. Nobody's there. She glances out the window to the parking lot, but the view is obstructed by a thin layer of ice. Then she takes a deep breath, steadies herself, and makes her way over to the staircase that leads down to the train tracks.

The hairs on the back of her neck are standing up, but she reminds herself there's a good chance she's overreacting —to all of it. And for a moment, she considers that she might be making the biggest mistake of her entire career.

Too late to second-guess myself now.

When she lifts her foot to start down the stairs, she freezes, reacting a split second too late to the sensation of a presence behind her. In an instant, she's flying headfirst in the air looking down at the cold, menacing metal stairs.

She closes her eyes and braces herself, incapable of emitting the terrifying scream that's welling up inside her.

ONE

CASSIE

I accepted this position last summer, in the wake of a gut-wrenching breakup. You'd think after he broke my heart, he would at least have been gentlemanly enough to offer to move out of our apartment and let me stay put.

But that's not how it happened. He reminded me that it was his apartment first, which is true. Then he offered me a small sum of money. And then he gave me a deadline to find a new place. It was all very businesslike.

"There's someone else?" I asked.

"Does it really matter?" he replied. "What's the point in doing this to yourself, Cassie?"

He tried to deny it at first, to spare me the sordid details. But I eventually got most of the story out of him. We'd been living together for over a year. Dating for over two. I thought we were "going somewhere." Our sex life had never been electrifying, but it was satisfying and comfortable, and that was enough for me.

When things cooled off a bit, about six months before he

dropped the bomb on me, I figured that was just how it was in a long-term relationship. I'd never lived with anyone before, so I had no frame of reference.

Then our silly little arguments stopped. He began to act polite—the way you interact with a relative stranger—like he didn't care enough to fight back. I felt something was up. Something had changed, but I didn't dare bring it up. I held my breath and waited to see if things would go back to normal.

I guess on some level a woman can sense when she's losing a guy, I just wasn't ready to face it. Because for me, getting involved with someone is a lot more complicated than it is for the average person. In hindsight, I suppose I can see that the relationship was never all that great. He probably did me a favor by ending it.

But it was all I had at the time, and I wasn't ready to let go. So when he told me that, yes, there was someone else, I felt like I'd been punched in the stomach. I have my pride, most of the time, but it seemed to be eluding me that day.

I'd like to say I held my head high and stormed out when he fessed up, but that's not what happened.

"You better be sure about this," I offered. "I don't give second chances."

"I'm in love with another woman. I'm sorry. It's over."

Then he turned from me and walked out the door.

So when I went to a conference in New York City the following week and learned about a teaching position at a boarding school thousands of miles from my California home that offered faculty housing, it seemed like it was meant to be. I could pocket my payoff from Evan, regroup, start over, and live happily ever after, following a proper but brief mourning period. I had just turned thirty so I didn't plan to pine away for too long.

Obviously, I wasn't thinking straight. I've stranded myself on top of a mountain in rural upstate New York, surrounded by acres of woods. A two-hour trek to New York City on a good day.

What was I thinking? Who am I going to meet here?

One thing I've learned from this experience is never make a major life decision in the midst of emotional turmoil.

I moved here from San Diego, totally unprepared for the insane winter weather we've been having here. Falcon Ridge Academy sits near the top of a medium-high peak of the Catskill Mountains on a plateau overlooking the Hudson River far in the distance.

It all looked so beautiful when I came to interview back in June. The day was clear and breezy, the setting a bucolic wonderland. I imagined long walks in the woods surrounded by vibrant fall colors where I would clear my head and heal my heart. A respite from the rat race. I'd write. I'd think. I'd grow stronger.

Now it's December, and the campus feels more like a minimum-security prison: isolated, creepy, and desolate. The walls of my four-hundred-square-foot apartment feel like they're closing in on me as the bare branches of the tree outside my bedroom window scrape at it with each gust of wind. Long, craggy fingers trying to claw their way inside.

From a distance, the structure I'm housed in seems to teeter on its foundation, threatening to tumble down the steep mountainside with every gust of wind. It's perilously close to the drop-off behind it. I was surprised that there's no real barrier there, aside from a row of stubby, round sage green shrubs that dot the perimeter of the grounds behind my building.

Winter arrived early, with a vengeance. And although the weather warmed up a bit today, there's still snow piled up outside from a "squall" last week. At least I'm learning some new vocabulary words. That's a blinding snowstorm that comes out of nowhere and makes it impossible to drive, see, or basically do anything, including walk from my apartment to the dining commons. I have no sense of direction. I'm sure I'll get lost and freeze to death or fall down the mountain before this winter is over. And it's just getting started.

Could this possibly get any worse?

But as I stare down at the alert on my phone, I realize I shouldn't have asked that question. They've called an emergency meeting of all faculty and staff that starts in twenty minutes. On a Sunday. And it's supposed to be my weekend off.

I thought we outlawed indentured servitude, but apparently not. For nine months of the year, they own me, and they know it. I forgo the primping—there's nobody to impress anyway—throw on some clothes, grab my jacket, and head out the door.

KIMI CHOY IS DEAD.

I heard our head of school say it, but it's not registering. I feel detached, like I'm watching a movie. I'm not sure if that's because I'm in shock or because I'm simply a terrible person. I was pretty close to her, at least until recently. Shouldn't I be feeling something?

Other people are reacting. I see a few eyes tearing up, but I can't seem to get my brain around it. The fact that this happened out of the blue. The fact that she was totally fine when I saw her Friday afternoon—and now she's gone. The fact that she died from a fall down the stairs at the Cortlandt train station.

Why did she go there, one of the most deserted stations around, and one that's at least twenty miles south of us? There are busier ones closer to our school she could have used.

And then I realize I'm probably in shock. I think back to when I arrived last August. Kimi was my department chair, and she went out of her way to make me feel welcome.

I'd never worked at a boarding school before, but she was a veteran. She was really friendly and offered some tips about where to get my hair cut and how to stay sane. She warned me that I would need to get some distance from the place on my weekends off. And she was really supportive when I told her about my break up and what a hard time I was having.

"I've got the perfect solution!" she said.

"What?"

"Let's go to the city for a night. Hit some of the trendy spots. Get you out there again."

"I don't think I'm ready to be 'out there,' Kimi."

"Oh, come on. It doesn't have to go anywhere. We'll get dressed up. Flirt a little. I could use some attention, too."

She had a point. Proximity to Manhattan was part of the

reason I took this job. I love it there, but I didn't realize how hard it would be to get into the city.

"Okay. Let's do it," I said. What did I have to lose?

We had a great time. Shopping. Bar-hopping. Most of it by ourselves, but we did mingle with a pair of older banker-type guys who seemed to enjoy the company of two "hot teachers." It didn't go anywhere, and I suppose we could have been offended by the comment. I needed an ego boost, though, and it worked to lift my spirits.

Our friendship cooled off a bit over the semester, and that's on me. Other teachers warned me off her, saying she was a sycophant, in tight with Brooke Baxter, the Dean of Faculty and our supervisor. Anything I told Kimi would get back to her, and Brooke is the type of administrator you need to vent about on a daily basis.

And now I feel guilty for going along with the crowd, for not giving Kimi the benefit of the doubt. It's possible she didn't have a choice.

Because the other teachers were right. Brooke Baxter is, at best, a power-hungry narcissist who'll stop at nothing to get ahead. At worst, she's a full-on manipulative psychopath. The woman hasn't bothered me much yet, but then I stay as far away from her as possible, and I hardly present as the weakest member of the herd. I'll do my time, save some money, and leave.

If Brooke got her hooks into Kimi, though, she may have felt her only option was to go along. It's possible she sought Kimi out because of her diffident demeanor. Like all mean girls, she preys on the weak ones.

I abandoned Kimi and left Baxter free to feast on her. And now I feel terrible about it. Kimi reached out to me the other day, in fact. She said she wanted to tell me something important. I told her I'd check my schedule and get back to her, but I never got around to it. I could have made time, but I didn't.

I feel truly horrible. I was weak, but it's like *Lord of the Flies* around here. The isolation of this place combined with the close proximity to a limited number of other adults who were strangers to me just a few months before creates a surreal atmosphere. Fitting in matters more here than in any setting I've been in since middle school. Alliances form out of necessity, like a nine-month-long season of *Survivor*.

Thinking back on my behavior and the way I cooled to Kimi, I finally start to feel something. Tears erupt and stream down my face as I admit to myself that I was a coward and a total shithead to her. And now I can never make amends because she's gone forever.

My tender moment comes to a halt when two police officers enter the auditorium and walk up to our new head of school, Doug Walker. He seems just as surprised to see them as I am. My stomach lurches and I sit up straight. I feel a tingling in the back of my scalp as I struggle to process what's happening.

I turn to the person next to me, an older cafeteria worker named Sharon who always calls me "dear." Her eyebrows rise as we lift our hands and shrug at one another.

What are police officers doing here? This was an accident.

Wasn't it?

I'VE BEEN HIDING in my apartment all day. I'm about to venture out to the gym, but I don't want to run into anyone. Our boarding population is pretty small, only about sixty students. They dine with us for lunch during the week, but they eat in their building on the weekends. Unless I'm on duty, I pretty much have the weekend to myself, and I don't see too many students, but it's impossible to avoid my coworkers unless I hibernate.

I know the gossip mill will be churning today. I'm not in the mood to engage, so I've been avoiding the other faculty members, which means I have nothing to eat besides cheese and crackers, the only food in my mini-fridge. I decide I might as well get a workout in before grabbing an early dinner, and I head out.

The school campus itself is fairly compact, less than a hundred acres, and houses several buildings. There's the dilapidated faculty apartment building where I live; the state-of-the-art student dorm and center on the opposite side of campus; the central, two-story building that contains the classrooms, gym, and faculty dining commons; and the exec-utive residences adjacent to the central building.

Calling the architecture eclectic would be a euphemism. The central building is old-school Gothic, made of brick and stone, the student center is modern and sleek, and the faculty dorm sits on the edge of campus like an afterthought: shabby, not chic, and fit only for the help.

As I'm walking to the gym, my mind is reeling. Is it possible that Kimi's death was foul play? Why else would the police come to the school? It's not like it happened here on campus.

The administration offered no explanation for the police officers. They simply wrapped up the meeting and dismissed us, so we are all left to speculate. And what people dream up on their own is usually so much worse than the truth. I wish they would level with us, although they might have their reasons for keeping things quiet. Maybe the police tied their hands.

I start to consider the implications, and I feel like my blood pressure is a little elevated. There's an energy in the air that wasn't here before—morbid curiosity mixed with fear—and an undercurrent of grief for those with a heart. Nothing happens here most of the time. It's not like living in a city where sensational news bombards people on a daily basis. The thought of a murderer in the area is terrifying yet titillating for some people but not for me.

I don't like being in the limelight. I like to keep a low profile, and not just because I feel out of place here. If they open up a murder investigation and question us, they might start prying into people's pasts. That's not good because I have something to hide.

And it needs to stay hidden.

MY ATTEMPT TO avoid other faculty members failed miserably, but it ended up being okay. After my workout, I shared a dinner table with some other faculty members. The mood was pretty somber. Even the two biggest Kimi-bashers looked remorseful.

It was surprisingly comforting to experience a shared sense of grief, and I decide to stop being so negative. My attitude is probably part of the problem. A major reason why I'm having such a hard time adjusting to this place.

I vow that I'll try to give people around here more of a chance. It's too late to make amends to Kimi, but at least I can learn something from the way I treated her.

The wind has picked up again and the temperature has plummeted. I can see my breath as I approach my building. I pull my collar tight around my neck. I'll be happy to get back into my room, even if it's not that warm.

It's dark already although it's not very late, and I long for the California sun as I enter the deteriorating structure, walk up the creaky steps, and get safely into my apartment.

Once inside, I hear the scraping of the tree branches on my window. I make a mental note to email the facilities team tomorrow to ask them to cut back the trees, but I'm not going to hold my breath. Falcon Ridge Academy is in a death spiral in terms of student enrollment, and I feel like it's on its last legs.

The boarding program relied a great deal on international students, and although that market has bounced back a bit, it's nothing like it was years ago. Even before the pandemic, they'd started to accept day students in an effort to fill seats, but that only kept things at a subsistence level.

The campus is in Ulster County, on the opposite side of the Hudson River from the train line to Grand Central Station, in an unincorporated hamlet with the same name as the school. A hamlet is a small village with no governing structure. The closest town is Plattekill. We rely on them as well as other nearby towns for our municipal services.

I'd never heard of a hamlet before I moved here. Most

people outside the state of New York probably haven't either. There are hundreds of them peppered throughout the vicinity. And it's apparently difficult to determine where many of them begin and end.

It seems very medieval to me, and I wonder what the implications are. What happens when we have an emergency? Do the various towns we rely on for ambulance or police service flip a coin for who comes? Most people don't seem to give it a second thought, so I keep these concerns to myself.

Although there are some pockets of wealth in the area, generally speaking, this isn't a very affluent area. Not many families around here can afford our tuition. As a consequence, we're struggling to stay afloat. That's probably why they keep it so freaking cold; I doubt there's much of a budget for tree pruning. I turn on the television, my only companion, get ready for bed, and count the days to winter break.

IF YOU ENJOYED THIS SAMPLE, *please see www. bonnietraymore.com for current retail availability.*